IVY COMPTON-BURNETT

A Father and his Fate

◄◄◄◆►►►

Introduced by
PENELOPE LIVELY

Oxford   New York
OXFORD UNIVERSITY PRESS
1984

Oxford University Press, Walton Street, Oxford OX2 6DP

London New York Toronto
Delhi Bombay Calcutta Madras Karachi
Kuala Lumpur Singapore Hong Kong Tokyo
Nairobi Dar es Salaam Cape Town
Melbourne Auckland

and associated companies in
Beirut Berlin Ibadan Mexico City Nicosia

Oxford is a trade mark of Oxford University Press

First published 1957 by Victor Gollancz Ltd
First issued as an Oxford University Press paperback 1984

British Library Cataloguing in Publication Data
Compton-Burnett, I.
A father and his fate.—(Twentieth-century classics).
—(Oxford paperbacks)
I. Title   II. Series
823'.912 [F]   PR6005.03895
ISBN 0-19-281853-8

Printed in Great Britain by
Richard Clay (The Chaucer Press) Ltd
Bungay, Suffolk

INTRODUCTION

BY PENELOPE LIVELY

Ivy Compton-Burnett's nineteen novels occupy a curious position in the spectrum of English fiction: maverick, *sui generis*, they are as remarkable for what they are not as for what they are. Detached both from public events and from recognizable landscapes, they concentrate on a Sartrean world: the enclosed torments of family life. The standard situation of a Compton-Burnett novel involves oppression, exploitation and rebellion. Violence predominates: mainly verbal, sometimes actual. In a world stripped of the intrusions of public existence husbands and wives, parents and children, masters and servants perform a subtle, comic and horrifying ceremony of insult and manipulation. It is like nothing else; her voice is unique, though echoes of its manner can be heard in Henry Green and of its accuracy in Barbara Pym. She has always been a special taste, attracting irritation from some quarters and passionate advocacy from others. But the extraordinary wit and force of her style are undeniable; she creates a world of her own, a world that is a luridly distorted and at the same time disconcertingly apt reflection of the real one.

The families who provide the casts of the novels exist in a state of detachment from the processes of history and the evocations of place. Public events are never mentioned; locations are seldom specified. Nearly all the books have the same setting: a large country house occupied by a family of disparate generations and complex relationships in the late Victorian period. The subject matter is the exercise of power. Various interpretations of Ivy Compton-Burnett's choice of so restricted a stage have been put forward, but the most potent one seems to be its absolute appropriateness for her purposes The extended Victorian family offered opportunities for the use and abuse of power unequalled since the baronial system: an emphasis on primogeniture, an attendant serf class by way of children and servants, concentration of economic resources in a single hand. Exclude distractions by way of wider social comment or the demands of employment, suspend the characters in time and place, and the way is open for an exact scrutiny of what they then say and do to each other. The weapons of personality and language are brought to bear against those of money and position. The result is tragedy—and comedy.

Ivy Compton-Burnett died in 1969, aged seventy-five. Her last novel, *The Last and the First*, was published posthumously; her first, *Dolores*, had appeared in 1911. *Dolores*, though, is an unsatisfactory book generally regarded as outside the main body of her work which begins with the publications of *Pastors and Masters* in 1925. All the novels are set between 1888 and 1902 (with the exception of *Pastors and Masters* which takes place in 1918). She herself is quoted as having said "I do not feel that I have any real or organic knowledge of life later than about 1910." The masterly first volume of Hilary Spurling's biography (the second appears in 1984) discusses the relation of the novels to the early circumstances of Ivy Compton-Burnett's life: enormous family, offspring of different mothers, the oppressive widowhood of Ivy's own mother, Ivy's tyranny over her younger sisters, the death of both of her brothers and suicide of two sisters. "I think that actual life supplies a writer with characters much less than is thought", she later said, ". . . people in life hardly seem to be definite enough to appear in print. They are not good or bad enough, or clever or stupid enough, or comical or pitiful enough." And indeed the essence of her characterization is exaggeration, that dramatizing and formalizing of personality that has led some critics to find her people unreal. If her own family appear in the novels, they do so with the poetic licence of distortion; more importantly, she drew, for ever after, on the traumas and claustrophobias of her own youth for the basic content of her fiction—the ways in which people live with those from whom they cannot escape.

A Father and his Fate displays Ivy Compton-Burnett's style at its most bleak and unadorned. Unlike the relatively discursive *Manservant and Maidservant*, perhaps her finest novel and one which provides considerable descriptive background and authorial comment, *A Father and his Fate* consists almost exclusively of dialogue. To read it is to have an eery sense of listening to disembodied voices, powerful and disturbing. This is the case with all the novels, but here it reaches an intensity that requires minute attention from the reader: for instance, the absence of authorial information often conceals a silent presence—there may be someone else in the room during a conversation who does not speak but whose listening ear is crucial to what is being said. Entrances and exits are as bluntly announced as in a play or, significantly, they may be so opaquely referred to that the reader can miss them. The book's structure is a symphony of voices; the narrative advances through the words of the participants and through them we learn what they are like. The petulant, self-justificatory tone of Miles Mowbray, the father, rapidly establishes itself in contrast to the astringent and occasionally sibylline remarks of his three daughters and the oblique commentaries of their male cousins, who act—as the young frequently do in a Compton-Burnett novel—as a kind of Greek chorus.

Children are used as symbols of powerlessness, in bondage to their parents and their condition. The three daughters in *A Father and his Fate* have not achieved the liberation of marriage and are denied that of employment by their social status—as miles, with devastating absence of tact, explains: "Would you have them go out as governesses, may I ask?" At which point we learn that Miss Gibbon, the girls' governess, is in the room. Miles, when gently reproved, blunderingly attempts to retrieve the situation (as he will continue to do, through a series of progressively more fatal insensitivities).

> ". . . She does not take my words to herself, or fancy they bear upon her. It does not need saying."
> "The words did not need it either," muttered Malcolm.

People frequently mutter. Malcolm, Miles's nephew and heir

(primogeniture or male inheritance are common Compton-Burnett plot ingredients), expresses his frustration and hatred with asides. His brothers, the Greek chorus, comment in this way; so do the three girls. Language is the only effective weapon of the weak, and Ivy Compton-Burnett frequently allows her oppressed characters the best lines. They may be helpless within the hierarchy, but within the context of the verbal violence that is at the heart of all the novels they often come out on top. In one of the lighter exchanges, Miles uses words of Christina Rossetti, denies that he has done so ("I never quote other people"), climbs down in the face of his daughters' quiet irony ("Well, I suppose the poet and I said the same thing"), and is further discomfited to learn the poet's sex, his views on the inferiority of women having been made abundantly clear from the early pages of the book.

For women, power is contingent upon marriage. For men, it is economic. Miles Mowbray, as head of the household, reigns; no-one disputes that it should be so, though several question his style of government. But, crucially to the story, his supremacy carries with it the additional weapon of bestowing secondary authority on a wife. At the outset, of course, he has one: Ellen, the mother of his daughters, is alive and well. And then, with typical disregard for the niceties of plot, Ivy Compton-Burnett despatches both Miles and Ellen on a journey, its purpose only vaguely specified, from which Miles returns alone, Ellen having apparently drowned in a shipwreck. And this sets in motion the action of the story: Miles instantly appropriates his nephew's fiancée, Verena (who has herself only recently appeared on the scene—the events of *A Father and his Fate* are precipitate even in Compton-Burnett terms), and announces his intention of marrying her. The daughters are confronted with the prospect of a stepmother their own age. "It is a Shakespearian state of affairs", comments Malcolm, resignedly accepting the loss of his future wife as, with the later twist of the plot, he is to calmly take her back again. His passive bitterness in the face of perfidy may make him seem a barely credible character, but in fact this is behaviour that crops up again and again in the novels.

Compton-Burnett people may rail eloquently against the evil meted out to them by others or by fate, but they often remain remarkably stoical in the face of reverses of fortune. And, just as the subject of the novels is the exercise of power, so the action frequently is concerned with switchbacks of circumstance: the humble are elevated, the mighty fall.

The central figure of *A Father and his Fate*, Miles, is one of Ivy Compton-Burnett's most successful domestic dictators in the marriage of comedy with sheer awfulness. He is a man of unswerving insensitivity, alternately celebrating his affection for his family and beating his brow over their alleged lack of consideration for him. But his finest moments are concentrated in the speeches of self-justification to which he treats everyone at each new revelation of the extent of his bad behaviour. "Is there nothing Uncle cannot carry off?", says his nephew Nigel at one point, with ironic admiration. "I imagined his position as impossible." For this is the point at which Ellen, revealed as alive after all, has returned home to be received lovingly by her husband, who had been on the verge of marrying a girl forty-four years younger than himself.

One cannot but feel that in fact Verena and Miles would have been appropriately paired. The orphan child of a friend, she has been taken in by Eliza, Malcolm's mother and Miles's sister-in-law, and reveals capacities of opportunism that would equip her well for a career in a Compton-Burnett household. First she gets herself engaged to Malcolm, then she dishes him for Miles, and then when Ellen's survival is revealed she makes a bid to save the situation by proposing to the daughters that this should be concealed and the marriage should proceed— bigamously. And when that fails she has one final move up her sleeve and brings the whole pack of cards down on Miles's head by revealing that he, too, had attempted to conceal Ellen's survival. But Miles is equal even to this, producing first a tortuous argument of justification for his actions and eventually falling back on an attitude of false humility: "I have had some hard experience, of a kind quite beyond your grasp. And I have done my best with it. And my best was only what it was. I am only what I am. I don't pretend to be anything else." It is a fine display of evasion and retrieval, and a dexterous shift from an earlier and more grandiose position:

> ". . . I seem to be destined not to live as other men."
> "So it was something as dignified as destiny," murmured Audrey. "And it need not be referred to Father at all."

The conversational formality of the novels is mirrored by formality of scene. One of the paradoxes relished by admirers of Ivy Compton-Burnett is the way in which the lurid matter of the stories—incest, bastardy, attempted murder—is revealed, more often than not, over the breakfast- or the tea-table. The quintessential Compton-Burnett scene is a meal-time, the occasion for the family to get down to the daily ritual of attack and counter-attack. In *A Father and his Fate* meal-times become occasions for the pointed discussion of relative power as demonstrated in the question of who shall sit where. The arrangement of the table is invested with as much significance as the line-up of the Kremlin at a May Day parade. Verena, displaced after Ellen's return, is able to harp upon her previous relationship with Miles by refusing to say how she likes her tea poured—"Miles can tell you."

It is in the course of this particular meal scene that one of the only physical props of the entire novel is mentioned—a silver teapot. And this is not done casually—the teapot has symbolic force; whoever wields it is in the seat of power. But for the rest, we are told nothing: we do not know what the house is like, or its surroundings, except that the estate includes a farm, and that the subsidiary household of Eliza and her sons is somewhere very close. We are given brief physical descriptions of the main characters, as in many of the novels, though the curious thing is that such is the force of their utterances that one instantly forgets them. They remain in the head not as flesh and blood but as manifestations of language—Miles's speeches of devious egotism, the wry and dry comments of Audrey, the awed irony of her cousins, the self-assertion and interference of Eliza.

The secondary and dependent household is another favourite

Compton-Burnett ingredient. The poor relations, displaced by the laws of inheritance or by accident of birth, stand on the fringes of the action, getting revenge, as often as not, by way of malign comment. Their situation may be intolerable, but they retain the weapons of guerrilla resistance: *sotto voce* observation, clandestine meddling, stirring-up of resentment. Eliza's method of manipulation and insertion of herself is to arrive, unannounced, at frequent intervals and usually at moments of heightened domestic tension, under the pretext of concern and desire to offer support. "I am sure Aunt Eliza is good at heart", says Constance at one point, to which Ursula replies, with fine ambiguity, "That is a hard thing to say." Much is made by Eliza of the fact that she is deprived of the presence of her eldest son by his situation in fief to his uncle: required to live in his uncle's house and manage the estate as heir apparent, though granted none of the privileges or concessions that such an heir might be expected to receive. Indeed, Eliza and Miles are a good match for each other in their emotional diatribes about the tribulations of parenthood and the huge debt of gratitude and obedience owed by the young. To be young, in an Ivy Compton-Burnett world, is to be the lowest of the low: dependent, powerless, biding one's time. It is impossible not to relate this view to the circumstances of her own youth, growing up in a household tyrannized by an embittered and headstrong woman, her own mother, whose style of dictatorial rule Ivy herself was to adopt after she had died leaving Ivy as head of the family.

Ivy Compton-Burnett's stylistic austerity has offended some of her critics, and in none of the novels is this manner more keenly demonstrated than in *A Father and his Fate*. Her situations and characters have been said to be "unreal", and indeed refinement of narrative is not one of her strengths: she can take a cavalier line with plot; melodrama is only a step away. But to base rejection of her work on its manner is to be impervious to its purpose. Like all major writers, she is performing at several levels: what is said, what appears to be said, what is not said. The richness and craft of her language give it an after-effect; it is often only when you arrive on the next page that you realize what has been conveyed on the previous one. The real meaning of the novels—the outraged sensibilities, the griefs, the stoicisms—lies beneath the language.

"I wonder if there is anyone in the world who cares for me," said Miles, leaning back in his chair. "I often ask myself that question."
"Then you should answer it," said Ursula. "It is less safe to put it to other people."

Compton-Burnett dialogue is peppered with this kind of double-edged response, sometimes capable of several different interpretations, so that to read, or to listen, is to experience just that sense of disorientation that those participating in such an exchange either feel or intend. The unreality of her world is a reflection of the uncertainty inherent in relationships: we say one thing but may mean another; words prevaricate. Equally, within the context of what she sets out to do—this exact examination of the weapons and manœuvres of domestic warfare—it is a strength rather than a failing to exclude all distractions by way of a defined world beyond the prison of the household. Heads of households may concern themselves briefly with the sources of their economic strength; no-one else so much as reads a newspaper. This may not be life as it seems to the reader, but it wonderfully concentrates attention on that aspect of life that interests the writer. For those who enjoy Ivy Compton-Burnett, narrative melodrama and patrician disregard for reality are endearing rather than irritating traits; you read to be enlightened about the ways in which people persecute those closest to them and how the persecuted respond—the pleasures to be derived are those attached to precise use of language. The style, in that sense, is the content. It is an acquired taste, and one that, once acquired, brings with it illuminations about language as well as about behaviour.

A FATHER AND HIS FATE

CHAPTER 1

"My DEAR, GOOD girls!" said Miles Mowbray. "My three dear daughters! To think I have ever felt dissatisfied with you and wished I had a son! I blush for the lack in me, that led me to such a feeling. I feel the blood mount to my face, as I think of it. I would not change one of you for all the sons in the world. I would not barter you for all its gold. And I am not much of a person for wealth and ease. I am happy as a countryman, husbanding the land his fathers held before him. I have not let any of it go from my hand. Not a foot has escaped to swell the holding of another. My brother's son will take it from me, as if he were my own. My brother has raised up seed unto me. I look to hear the words, 'Well done', from him, if ever a man has heard them from the lips of another. What do you say, Malcolm?"

"Am I to repeat the words, Uncle? I can hardly improve on them."

"Is it from a brother that we hope to hear them?" said the eldest girl. "Father is exalting his family."

"Oh, I am no theologian. I am no person for thrusting each word into a settled place. A broad survey of a matter is the thing for me. Is it not for you, my wife?"

"I am willing to think it is."

"And it is, my Ellen. I can vouch for it. No one breathes who can meet a question with a wider view. You would not have driven anyone to the stake. I can imagine you going there yourself. Ah, I can see that. Head up, hands clenched, resolve in every line of your face and form! How I can see it!"

"And with some pleasure, it seems," said his daughter.

"With some pride, my Ursula. Ah, with some pride. If there is anyone who understands your mother, it is I. Twenty-six

3

years I have lived with her and watched her day by day. Ah, I have every aspect of her stamped on my mind.''

"And it seems some extra ones," said his wife. "I might send someone to the stake as willingly as go myself. Not that I can imagine either.''

"Well, my girls, what do you say of yourselves? Would you be ready to stand for your faith? Put yourselves in the martyrs' place and tell your father.''

"We should have to have a faith first," said Ursula.

"Of course you would have to have a thing, before you could suffer for it. Why say what goes without saying? We do not want cynicism and self-complacence here. We have enough of them all around us. I would not rank myself on the side of things so commonplace. I hold to the beliefs that have their own life and do their own work. And I am not afraid to say so.''

"He really is not," murmured Malcolm. "Would he have considered the stake?''

"I hope I should be able to hold firm," said the second daughter, in a quiet, aloof tone, as if to herself.

"And you would, my resolute girl. Constance you would be in name and nature. If anyone is sure of it, it is your father.''

"I wish I could be sure of myself, Father.''

"I could not go to the stake," said the third daughter. "Or do anything that corresponds to it.''

"Neither could I," said her mother. "It somehow seems to be a safeguard.''

"Neither could I," said Malcolm. "Uncle and Constance would have to go together.''

"Oh, well, I am not sure about that," said Miles, looking down. "I might not hold fast when the moment came. I see that the spirit might be willing but the flesh weak.''

"Nothing in me would be willing," said Audrey.

"It is hardly a pressing question for any of us," said Malcolm. "But when it arises, it should not find us unprepared.''

"Ah, you are an upright creature, Ellen," said Miles, leaning back in his chair. "You would not disguise the truth to exalt yourself. There are few of us of whom that can be said."

"I hope more than you think, Father," said Constance.

"Does Uncle mean he is not one of them?" said Malcolm.

"Well, I may not be. I said it was true of few of us. I hardly suppose you are one yourself."

"I do not care what people think of me."

"Oh, that is a thing so often said, that it means nothing. I pay no heed to it."

"I hardly think I care much," said Ursula.

"Well, you may not, being as you are. What about you, my Constance?"

"I hope I act up to what I should like them to think, Father."

"I believe I assume that they think it," said Ellen.

"And you are right, my wife. In your case there could be no question. What about my little Audrey?"

"I believe I do the same, Father. Most of us have two views of ourselves. One our own, and one to share with other people."

"Ah, you are an honest company. As different from Malcolm and me as you can be, I daresay. I believe women are more straightforward than men. Though they are held to be so underhand and sly. And there cannot be smoke without flame, of course."

"I am sure they are not underhand, unless they have to be," said Constance.

"Few people would be so without reasons," said Ursula. "An upright person would be upright in spite of them."

"Well, I have known many instances of that."

"Have you known many instances of anything?" said Malcolm.

"What do you mean?" said Constance.

"You can hardly have met them in the life you have led."

"What life?" said Miles, looking up. "Would you have them go out as governesses, may I ask? Would you have them earn their bread? I despise a father who allows his daughters to do such things. I hold him unworthy of the name of a man. I wonder you can sit and say such a thing before your aunt."

"It did make me remember that I was in the room," said Ellen, smiling.

"Father," said Constance in a low tone, "you know Miss Gibbon is here."

"Is she? Well, of course she is, when we are here ourselves, and she is one of us. She does not take my words to herself, or fancy they bear upon her. It does not need saying."

"The words did not need it either," muttered Malcolm.

"No, I did not refer anything to myself, Mr. Mowbray. We all have different lives, of course. It is only natural."

"And my girls have the one they ought to have. A life in the family home, with the protection and provision that is fit for them. What more could they want?"

"There are other things," said his nephew.

"And if they had them, what would it come to? A family home over again. And I daresay a less good one."

"But one of their own, Uncle."

"Well, whose is this but theirs? You have not come into it yet. You talk as if I were a tyrant and they were martyrs."

"You are fond of the idea of martyrs. Things are not as good as that. A martyr incurs his suffering of his own will and for a cause."

"Incurs suffering! Whatever is in your mind? The house is not a torture chamber."

"Then it is different from many houses. My mother's has many features of one."

"Well, well, your mother is a woman by herself, as we are all agreed. But she has great qualities, has Eliza. She is built on a big scale. You are fortunate in your mother, Malcolm, even if there is the other side."

"People are not often fortunate, when that is so," said Ursula.

"I think the idea of martyrdom ought to be more with us," said Constance.

6

"Why do you think   ?" said Audrey. "It seems to be our most frequent one."

"Well, Malcolm, would you like to read prayers this morning?" said Miles. "Would it get you into the spirit for the day? I think you could do with the help."

"No, I should not, thank you, Uncle."

"Suppose I ask you to read them?"

"Then I must refuse your request."

"I wish you to read them," said Miles, in another tone. "I direct you as the head of the house to obey me in the matter."

"I cannot render you obedience."

"You mean you will not?"

"Yes, I mean that, Uncle."

"Do you not recognise my authority?"

"No, I am a man of twenty-six."

"I suppose you are afraid of looking foolish," said Miles, in an easier manner, but with a change in his eyes.

"Everyone is afraid of that," said Ursula. "And you seem to be contemplating it, Father."

"You feel self-conscious about it?" said Miles to his nephew.

"So you had a reason for suggesting it."

"My reason was the one I gave, that I thought it might help you through your day. You did not seem in the temper for it. And it is steadying to read the words of truth to ears ready to receive them."

"Well, I will not deprive you of the aid."

"Oh, there is that note again, the touch that besmirches everything. Talk that has no meaning, uttered with an eye to effect! Now am I to repeat my words or am I not?"

"I can only repeat mine, Uncle."

"Well, you will not do so. I am glad you do not dare. I am glad you cannot look me in the face and utter them. Why should you live as the son of the house, if you cannot take my mantle on your shoulders sometimes? The day will come when you must take it entirely. I wish the place was not entailed in the male line. I wish one of my girls could inherit it. I do so from my heart. And I make no secret of it."

7

"It is a natural wish," said Ellen. "There is no need to make it a secret. It could hardly be one."

"I have no desire to bruit my feeling abroad. I am content to keep it to myself. Have I not always done so? Have I not accepted Malcolm as my heir, treated him as my successor? And have I not a right to be obeyed by a nephew dealt with in that way? He would not disobey his mother."

"That is true," said Malcolm. "It is why I was willing to leave her house. I am past the age for taking orders."

"Oh, you must obey before you can command, you know. Everyone knows that."

"Is it always true?" said Ellen. "The same person may not be good at both."

"And so many are good at commanding," said Audrey. "There seem to be too few to take the commands."

"And Malcolm would like to be the first," said Miles. "Well, he will not be in my house. The time has not come for it. Now, Malcolm, take that Bible and do as I said. Do you hear?"

"Yes, I do," said Malcolm, protecting his ear with his hand. "No one could fail to. But for God's sake not before the servants, Uncle."

"And for all our sakes," said Ursula to her sisters.

"Well, you can do something else before the servants," said Miles, lowering his voice as the latter entered, and speaking as if he suggested some humiliation. "You can sit and listen to one of your cousins reading. You can do that before them. And you will do it and give your mind to it. Do you understand?"

Malcolm kept his hand to his ear. Constance half-rose with a resolute air and a look towards her father. Ellen took the Bible from him, and, moving to his seat, conducted the usual ceremony.

"Now what is the meaning of that?" he said, when the servants had gone.

"If neither you nor Malcolm will read prayers, it is for me to do it. There is no reason for the girls to be called on."

"No, but somehow I think of Ursula as coming after me. It is because she would have done so, if she had been a son. I should have liked to think of my daughter in my place."

"You seem to do so," said Malcolm. "And to let your thoughts skirt over me."

"Oh, don't be such a young coxcomb. You might be six instead of twenty years older. Do you suppose I should recognise your position as I do, if my thoughts skirted over you, as you put it? You ought to wear skirts yourself. That would be the thing for you."

"Sometimes I half-suspect you of not thinking women equal to men, Father," said Constance.

"Half-suspect me! Why, what is the harm in that? You can do it wholly if you like. Of course women are not equal to men. They are not so strong or intelligent. That is, they have their own kind of intelligence. And a more important kind, of course. But they are not the same. Naturally they are different. Yes, you may laugh, Ellen. I know you think you are cleverer than I am. And you may be, for all I can say. Of course you are. We all recognise it. And if there is anyone who does so, it is your husband."

"Is there so much difference between men and women, Mr. Mowbray?" said Miss Gibbon. "Except in the matter of bodily strength. Surely mental quality depends on the individual."

"Ah, you are right, Miss Gibbon. You are right," said Miles, stroking his moustache.

The family gathered at the breakfast table: Ellen at its head, a tall, simply handsome figure, with a fair, simply handsome face and an expression that somehow belied it; Miles at the bottom, shorter and darker than his wife, with thick, broad hands and face and figure, and small, pale, restless eyes; the daughters at the sides, Ursula resembling her father, but with more looks, Constance her mother, but with less, Audrey a cross between the two; and their cousin tall and spare and sallow, with a rougher cast of feature and a consciously cynical glance. Miss Gibbon looked as alien a

9

figure as she had fifteen years before, when she had been described by Miles on Ursula's tenth birthday as a birthday gift, and was hardly sure of being seen as more of a gift now than then. She was a small, sober, silent woman, with a quality of escaping notice, and a less recognised one of taking it. Her ordinary, honest face had few expressions, or did not show those it might have had. She had a useful past to look back on, kept her eyes from the future, and assumed she was happy in the present, as she wished it might go on for ever. Her age of forty-nine seemed a settled part of her, and indeed had ceased to change, all that could be done to keep time at a standstill. Ellen liked and trusted her. The sisters gave her a sort of friendship. Miles paid her spasmodic tribute, and Malcolm hardly knew whether she was in the room or not. The problem of what her duties would be, when her pupils were grown, was imminent; and Audrey was kept in the schoolroom at nineteen in order to postpone it. And although Miss Gibbon's age had become stationary, Audrey's had not.

"I wonder if there is anyone in the world who cares for me," said Miles, leaning back in his chair. "I often ask myself that question."

"Then you should answer it," said Ursula. "It is less safe to put it to other people."

"Ah, it is indeed. I have found that," said Miles, with a grimness of his own.

"If you impersonate King Lear, Father," said Constance, "you must be prepared to see us in the other characters."

"Well, I am sure I should not mind. I should be glad of some show of feeling, whether it was real or not. Even empty words are better than nothing."

"That may be true," said Ellen. "I think it often is. But they are not much better."

"I do not think you mean what you say, Father," said Constance.

"Well, I meant it for the moment. Upon my word I did. A wave of isolation swept over me. I felt I was alone in the world, with my wife and children about me. If anyone has

10

known the meaning of the words, 'alone amongst many', I knew it then. Do you ever have a feeling like that, Miss Gibbon? Well, I suppose you always have it. I mean, you are not with your own family, of course."

"That is not found to prevent it," said Audrey.

"No, Mr. Mowbray, but our background is behind us. We do not know what it is to be without it."

"Well, I have simply what you see," said Miles, spreading his hands with a faint air of complacence.

"So has everyone here," said Ursula.

"Ah, but your mother has more. She has the things that lie beneath. You all feel more deeply for her. Even Malcolm does so in his heart. I am not saying she does not deserve it. I am simply stating the truth. There is no comparison. What would you say, Miss Gibbon?"

"I think I should say that comparisons are odious, Mr. Mowbray."

"My Audrey, do you love your father? You are my Cordelia, you know."

"Then you know the risk you are taking."

"Yes, that is sure to be said. And so I am left without a word. That is what would happen to me. I did not expect anything else. Always some excuse to leave me high and dry, a forgotten hulk on the strand! Well, I am learning to suffer it. I expect nothing. I ask for nothing. I would accept nothing. I go my way alone."

"In a sense we all do that," said Audrey.

"We may remember that you would accept nothing, Father," said Constance, gravely.

"Oh, yes, reduce me to the common level. I am not to stand an inch apart. I am to belong to the herd."

"In a sense we all do that too."

"In what sense? Do you think you belong to it? How would you like it to be thought?"

"We ought not to want to stand too far apart."

"Well, we all like to have a place of our own. And of course I know I have it. I don't know what I am talking about."

"I do," murmured Malcolm. "Himself."

"And whom else would you talk about? Or think about anyhow?"

"We must all do both sometimes," said Constance.

"Yes, of course we must, as I am doing. But I don't know what has come to me. Of course I am content to be amongst you all, to be one of you, to stand with those dear to me. I would not do anything else. I don't know what I was saying."

"Other people do know, Father. We must just try to forget it."

"Oh, forget it or not, as you like," said Miles, drumming his fingers on the table. "Would you like to have three daughters, Miss Gibbon?"

"What I have had is three pupils, Mr. Mowbray. And they have been enough for me."

"But you must have imagined other things. You must have imagined yourself married. Every woman has done so."

"Well, I daresay I did when I was young. I thought the fairy prince would come along, and forgot about him as I grew older. I think that happens to a good many of us."

"Perhaps it was the fairy prince who forgot," murmured Audrey.

"What did you say?" said Miles.

"Oh, nothing, Father."

"Come, you should not whisper. Tell us what you said."

"I said it was perhaps the fairy prince who forgot," said Audrey, in a distinct tone, as though he should have what he insisted on.

"Ah, well, I suppose he did. Ah, ha! Well, I suppose so. I don't know, of course. What do you say to it, Miss Gibbon?"

"I have already said, Mr. Mowbray. I forgot about him, as I grew older."

"Well, that was only fair, as he forgot about you. Perhaps you had no need of each other."

"We are none of us finding his memory good," said Ursula.

"You can only see that yours are no better, as Miss Gibbon did," said Malcolm.

"If she really did," said Miles. "Well, she did, of course. And I sympathise with her. We can grasp too much at these things. I should not welcome anyone who came to take a girl of mine. I should ask him to keep his distance, unless I was very sure of him."

"I certainly have no wish to marry," said Constance.

"Have you any great wish to be single either?" said Ursula.

"The change is less than is thought," said Ellen. "A family becomes a normal part of life. It gives no sense of difference."

"A normal part of life may not be a thing to dispense with," said Malcolm.

CHAPTER II

"WELL, YOU ARE all here," said Miles. "I am glad not to have to send for you. It seems a good augury for the hour before us. It may be a hard one. I have a hard thing to say. I must summon my courage to say it, and you must summon yours to hear. You know that your mother and I are soon to cross the seas, to look into the family affairs. You know I have been anxious about them. Well, they are worse than I thought. The truth is that the position is grave. Great care will be needed. Great retrenchment must be made. And I want to know in what way each of you is prepared to help. I am not asking for sympathy. I am offering none. I ask for something different. We have to deal in sterner things. I shall do my best. How will you do yours?"

There was only a short silence.

"So you have been worried, Father," said Constance. "I think we might have known. I am glad you are trusting us at last."

Miles waited with a half-smile.

"I do not want any more teaching," said Audrey. "That need hardly be said. Miss Gibbon could perhaps do things that would save expense."

"Oh, come, we are never too old to learn," said her father.

"But we may be too old to learn from someone who has always taught us."

"But that should make you grateful to her."

"Yes, but it does not alter my present age."

"Mr. Mowbray, I have reached a proud moment," said Miss Gibbon, with a startled expression. "It is the high-water-mark in a teacher's life, when a pupil has gone beyond her. And now it has come to me, I should make the most of it."

14

"Well, you must make the best of it. It has come, I suppose, if you agree."

"She will scarcely make too little of it," muttered Malcolm.

"I can manage anything that Audrey needs," said Ursula. "It will hardly be much. She reads a great deal alone."

"I can help her with her music," said Constance. "I have gone a good way myself."

"And do you think Audrey is my only liability?" said Miles, still smiling. "And at whose expense would you really be making these changes? Can you suggest nothing that does not displace our good friend, Miss Gibbon? I was thinking of things that depended really on yourselves."

"I could undertake your accounts," said Ursula. "I could get some system into them. I know it needs doing. And Malcolm would be glad of help."

"I could manage the organ in church," said Constance. " You bear the expense of the organist. It would not be a change for the worse. And we could even help in the house and save service. There is a good deal that Everard does, that we could do ourselves."

"And what would you do, Malcolm?"

"What I do now. Give my time to managing the place. I have none over."

"My dear, good girls!" said Miles, in a rather forced tone, as if the scene had hardly reached his expectations. "My always dear daughters! I knew I was safe in putting you to the test. I knew you were equal to it. But I need not keep you to your word. Things are not as I said. Your father was being King Lear again. And he has met a full response. He will cross the seas, leaving behind what is precious indeed. Malcolm, you must guard them for me. They are now doubly dear."

"I hardly know what they could have said, Uncle."

"They could have said many things. They could have said nothing. They could have done less and said the kind of thing you did."

"They could not have said it with truth."

"Well, I doubt if you did that yourself."

"Their sacrifices were hardly on a heroic scale."

"They were on their own. They would have done what they could. Who can do more?"

"Father, were you deliberately giving a wrong impression?" said Constance. "I will not use a stronger word."

"Why will you not?" said Malcolm.

"I was," said Miles. "I felt I was justified. And the result proves it."

"There may be other results," said Ellen.

"You took a risk, Father," said Ursula.

"I took none. I knew you, if you did not know yourselves."

"You have taken another," said his wife. "That of their not believing you in future."

"That risk is mine, and I care nothing for it. They will see it is no great one. They trust their father."

"Well, you trust them, Miles."

"Mr. Mowbray," said Miss Gibbon, in a pleasant tone, "if you would find it convenient to part from me, you would not hesitate to say so?"

"Indeed I should. I should do more than hesitate. Wild horses would not drag it from me. I could not utter the words. You are one of ourselves. We rise and fall together."

"I am glad we are not to fall," said Audrey. "And I am glad the question of my freedom has been raised and settled. I am sure Miss Gibbon would rather do different things."

"Yes, I think you have brought that about, Miles," said Ellen.

"And I am an adaptable person," said Miss Gibbon, correctly foreseeing her future.

"Well, Miss Gibbon can do different things then. She can be our general helpmate. There is nothing against that, if she sees nothing."

"And I can manage the organ," said Constance. "I think it would be as well. And Ursula will do the accounts. She has wanted to reorganise them."

"Now I did not mean you to set about hurting everyone's

16

feelings and pushing people out of their place. Miss Gibbon consents to fill another. Then that is well enough. But there is no need for matters to go further. They can stop there."

"What is it, Everard?" said Ellen, as the butler hovered near. "Do you want me for anything?"

"Well, may I say a word to you, ma'am?"

"Yes, if you need to. What is it?"

"If the young ladies can fill my place, ma'am, my service is not requisite. I should hardly wish to stay where I am a fiasco."

"Fiasco! What nonsense!" said Miles. "No one is filling your place. Let us hear no more of it."

"And if there is to be one change, ma'am, it is felt there can be another. In case the next thing should be that Cook was superfluous."

"And the gardener too, I suppose," said Miles, "and both the stable boys. Well, of all the nonsense! Miss Gibbon sets you an example."

"So I understand that you wish us to remain, ma'am?" said Everard, his eyes not leaving Ellen.

"Yes, of course you do," said Miles, "if you understand anything."

"And we should not look for reaction, ma'am? There would not be consequences?"

"No, it means nothing. The master was playing a trick on us. We are all to forget it."

"Thank you, ma'am. But many a true word is spoken in jest."

"Well, go and give the message to Cook seriously," said Miles. "And do not repeat what you hear in future."

"Not pass it on, sir?" said Everard, raising his brows. "I should be considered close."

"Well, be as open as you please on this occasion. Miss Gibbon, I am grateful to you. I wish they were all on your level."

Everard glanced at Miss Gibbon and smoothly left the room. He was a heavy, pale young man, with an air of aloofness that came from his possessing the quality. He served the family without any sign of interest. And it was a matter it was hardly possible to broach to him.

"Well, it is the level that makes the difference, Mr. Mowbray," said Miss Gibbon.

"Yes, of course there is no comparison," said Miles, uncertain if he had made one. "That need not be said. Well, Ellen, there is an end of it all. So let there be an end."

"It was you who made the beginning, Father," said Constance.

"It has not been a success, Uncle," said Malcolm.

"Not a success? I don't know what you mean. How could it have been more so?"

"Perhaps it hardly deserved to be," said Constance. "It was a strange thing to do, Father."

"It was a natural thing enough. There are all kinds of examples in books of people's being put to the test. I mean in the great classics. And it is due to people to let them show what they are, if you can depend on it. And I have let my daughters show it. And if they are now to prove it in another way, if the last sacrifice is to give up their sacrifices, they will be equal to it."

"I shall not be," said Audrey.

"In other words they were making none," said Malcolm.

"Well, I do not want things put in other words. That means in your words. My own words are good enough for me. Where are you going?"

"To visit my mother. I have not seen her for a week."

"And you don't dare to stay away any longer," said Miles, with grim sympathy. "No, I do not suppose you do. I should not in your place. I admire the way you have broken away and determined to steer your own course. It must have needed courage.'

"It needed many things."

"And that most of all. Ah, I know it did. There is no one on this earth, whom I would not rather set myself against than your mother. I wondered how your father could undertake her. I put it in plain words. 'My dear brother,' I said, 'you are a braver man than I am.' But he heard no reason. And the marriage was a success. Believe it or not, it was."

"I believe it," said Malcolm. "I was a witness of it. It lives in my memory. It casts its shadow over us. It was so great a success that nothing else can be so. No one can love her enough, admire her enough, give her enough. She can never be satisfied. And my brothers give a good deal."

"As you did before you left her. I remember, and I don't suppose you forget. Ah, Eliza takes her toll. And I have paid my share. I would not look her in the face and disagree with her, unless I had wife or daughter with me. It may not sound a manly thing to say, but there it is. And I daresay that to give a woman her head is the truest manliness."

"Then she has several manly relations," said Constance, with a compression of her lips.

"Ah, you do not care for your aunt, Constance. You have never taken to her. You hardly do her justice."

"I hope I recognise her good qualities, Father."

"Tell us what they are," said Audrey.

"Everyone recognises them," said Ellen, smiling. "They are too much afraid of not doing so. And she seems to have more than she ought."

"And she really has," said Ursula. "So we cannot entirely dislike her. Something about her prevents it. I almost understand why Uncle Malcolm was in love with her."

"Well, I don't understand that," said Miles. "I cannot say that I do. But I admire you for giving her her due, Ursula. It is not always that one woman does that to another."

"I should have thought women were fairer to women than men are, Mr. Mowbray," said Miss Gibbon. "I have known several men who recognised the tendency."

"Well, I daresay they are. I know what you mean. Men may be jealous of women. I have met cases of it. I have thought myself that too much allowance was made for them. When they seemed to have all that men have and more besides."

"It would surely be a very small man, who was jealous of a woman," said Constance.

"Would it?" said Ursula. "I have felt jealous of men. Does that mean I am a small woman? Or are women always small? Anyhow it seems to me that men have the best of things."

"Why, we could not meet a more esteemed person than your mother," said Miles. "Or than yours, Malcolm, if we happened to want to meet her. I am not myself, when I am with her. I find her somehow too much. If that is being jealous of her, then I am jealous. Though I would not be a woman myself. I admit it."

"I think I would rather be a woman than a man," said Constance.

"I would rather be a man," said Ursula.

"So would I," said Malcolm.

"Well, so would I," said Miles, in an open tone. "I do think it is the better thing. I mean the more advantageous, the better for the person concerned, the more selfish, if you please. And so I would choose it for myself, as anyone would."

"Which would you rather be, Mother?" said Constance.

"It is late to reconsider the position. And surely I have done too well as a woman to regret being one."

"And so you have, my dear one," said Miles, more loudly. "And which would my Audrey choose to be?"

"I think it is easier to be a woman. She has more allowance made for her. Being ordinary does not matter so much."

"I think that is rather acute, Mr. Mowbray," said Miss Gibbon. "My pupil does me credit."

"And so she does, Miss Gibbon. And so do they all. I wish they were still your pupils. And which would you choose to be?"

"Well, I have not had the choice, Mr. Mowbray. And I am content with my life and what I have done in it."

"We are confusing two questions," said Constance. "Which is better, a man or a woman? And which is it better to be? They are not the same."

"They may be the opposite," said Audrey. "I think they tend to be."

"Well, I should have thought they were the same in a way," said Miles. "But I daresay a woman is better. I am prepared to grant it. She is readier to sacrifice herself than a man. She is supposed almost to like doing so. And sometimes we can only hope she does. I trust it is true of you, Miss Gibbon, because it will have to be. You will be tossed about from pillar to post, and asked to do this and go thither, and never know whether you have an object in life or not. We are grateful to you for accepting the position. And we ought to be."

"She will have an object when we are away," said Ellen. "She will be in my place."

"Oh, well, my dear, Ursula is twenty-five."

"Yes, but she is no more."

"Well, Malcolm, I hope you will have an eye on them. On Miss Gibbon as well as your cousins. If she is in your aunt's place, you will be in mine. And there will be your mother as well. You will have enough on your shoulders. I doubt if a woman could support as much. I think more would be made of it."

Miles left the room, and Constance looked gravely after him.

"Do you think Father's ruse was justifiable, Mother?"

"Well, he revealed it too soon for the matter to be a great one."

"There was something childish about it. I think there is something childish about many men."

"And about many women. People have no chance to grow up. A lifetime is not long enough."

"How old are you, Mother, if I may ask?"

"I was sixty-three last birthday."

"You married late," said Ursula. "It looks as if we may do the same."

"Or as if there may be a further postponement," said Malcolm, as he followed his uncle.

"I hardly think Malcolm is improving," said Constance. "Or there has been no sign of it to-day."

"There never is, when he is going to his mother," said Ursula. "Though it might be a reasonable precaution."

"It is hard to live in two homes," said Ellen. "It is a strain on him, as it would be on anyone. And it puts a certain strain on us all."

"Sometimes I feel that too little is asked of us in our home," said Constance.

"There will be more in time. Your father and I will get older."

"But people may gain with the years," said Miss Gibbon. "Just as a face can be enhanced by its experience. I have met many cases of it."

"Where have you met them?" said Audrey.

"Well, there is one before our eyes."

"Mother, you are being flattered," said Constance.

"Indeed she is not," said Miss Gibbon. "And I am sure you do not think so."

"I might have said she was receiving a deserved compliment."

"You must be careful," said Ellen. "I may get to expect them. And that would make a demand."

"Not if they were spontaneous," said Miss Gibbon.

Ellen left the room to escape attention, but was followed by the giver of it.

"I am glad Miss Gibbon has something in her life," said Constance. "Her feeling for Mother makes a thread running through it. It is hard to see what she would have without it."

"I should have thought it was easy," said Audrey. "She would have nothing."

"And you do not feel she deserves much," said Ursula. "That is how we see people who have taught us. They have had to reveal themselves."

"Well, they may think it of people they have taught. They also are not unrevealed. When she wanted an object for her feeling, she did not turn to us."

"I think she sees us with affection," said Constance.

"I think she assumes she does," said Ursula. "Fifteen years must have had some result."

"She is perhaps hardly educated enough for a governess."

"Well, if she was, she would not be one. That is why governesses are not educated."

"Sometimes I almost wonder why Mother engaged her."

"She was suitable for us when we were young. And then she could not be got rid of without being dismissed."

"And Father would not have that. And we should think less of him, if he would."

"And he does not think education necessary for daughters. He has said he did not intend us for governesses."

"I am sure any element of dishonesty on Miss Gibbon's part has been unconscious."

"Well, dishonesty may be that. It is honesty that never is. I suppose it takes too much effort. It is too unnatural."

"It is made easy for most of us," said Audrey. "But I should yield to temptation."

"People always do," said Ursula. "If they resist it, it is something else."

"I do not agree," said Constance. "I am sure there are many instances of heroic resistance of it."

"If you are thinking of martyrs, I hardly believe they were tempted. If they had not been martyrs, they would have been nothing. And that tempts no one."

"It tempts me," said Audrey. "And I am going to yield."

"I wonder if this is a thing I ought to say," said Constance, looking down. "I sometimes feel a sort of surprise that Father and Mother came together."

"I always feel surprise at people's marriages," said Ursula. "I never follow their need of each other."

"Just as Constance cannot follow Mother's need of Father," said Audrey.

"I did not mean to be so plain. And I believe Father had his attraction as a younger man."

"And that is being less plain?"

"I wish I had not said anything. It is never wise to say these things."

"You yielded to the temptation."

"Luncheon is on the table, Miss Ursula," said Everard, before Constance could yield further.

"So you were prepared to leave us, Everard."

"Well, miss, I did not instigate it. It was the idea that my office was a sinecure."

"I should have thought that might be a pleasant one."

"I have feelings, miss. And self-respect is not absent."

"Well, my three dear girls," said Miles, as they joined him. "Now let our last days together be days of joy and peace. Let no hard word or look escape us to mar the memory. Let us be lovely and pleasant in our lives. . . ."

"You are spilling the sauce over your arm, sir," said Everard at his elbow.

"Oh, it is your infernal way of holding the dish."

"Father, remember what you said," said Constance.

"Oh, yes, you had to say that. You could not let it pass. Well, I might not have, myself. Ah, ha! Well, I suppose I am not being what I said."

"But I think you are," said Ursula.

"So do I," said Audrey.

"Yes, well, I think so too," said Constance, after a pause. "Perhaps I might not have said what I did. Many of us would be put out by having our words brought up against us."

"Oh, I am not so easily overset. It is Malcolm who brings it about. And yet I miss him when he is not here. I am as inconsistent as the rest."

"I suppose I am too," said Constance. "I am both glad and sorry that we are not to have those extra duties."

"Oh, you wanted the change," said Miles, indifferently. "The duties would soon have palled."

"They are perhaps not variety in its best form," said Ursula.

"Well, I don't know what you do all day, and that is the

truth. I daresay you hardly know yourselves. But there is no need for you to know. So it should not trouble us."

"I know," said Audry. "We do nothing."

"Oh, I manage to make occupation for myself," said Constance. "Little things arise from hour to hour. And they cannot be called nothing."

"They can," said Audrey. "I call them that."

"You do not count, you chit," said Miles. "Go back to Miss Gibbon, if you want to fill your time."

"I do not want to. I shall like to have it free."

"Then what are you complaining about?"

"I am not doing so. It was before, that I complained."

"I am not available any longer, Mr. Mowbray," said Miss Gibbon, easily. "My mind is full of tasks that I may fulfil. I think the position of Jack-of-all-trades will suit me."

"And suit other people better," said Miles. "And better still, as time goes on."

"Can I do anything for you now, Mrs. Mowbray?" said Miss Gibbon, as Ellen rose.

"Yes, several things that I do less well myself. I have not out-distanced you like Audrey."

"I have been saying, Father," said Constance, "how fortunate it is that Miss Gibbon is so devoted to Mother. It makes a thread through her life."

"Ah, it is the thread through all our lives. It binds us to her, as it binds us to each other. It gathers the lives into a whole. Without it they would fall apart."

CHAPTER III

"Why, my son, it is a week since we saw you. We wondered if anything was wrong."

"You could have found out," said Malcolm, stooping to his mother's greeting. "You could have sent a message."

"It is hardly for us to do that. We assume we shall be told, if anything happens."

"Then you might have inferred that nothing had. It would be a safe conclusion. Nothing does."

"Well, it is good to see you. My home seems strange to me without my eldest boy. And things bear heavily on me, with the other two so young. I miss my companion-son. Now are you not coming to speak to them? Have you nothing to say to each other after a week?"

"We are held by the constraint of the parting. They find a strange brother has returned to them."

"From the great unknown," said the third son. "And indeed Uncle's house is that."

"You are silly boys," said Eliza, in mingled annoyance and pride. "I daresay you talk more freely when I am not here. Your mother puts a check on you. And there is no harm in that. But have you no news at all, Malcolm? Something must have happened in seven days."

"Perhaps that is what Uncle thought. Because he devised something. He spun a tale about ruin and retrenchment. And when he had made the girls rise to the occasion, revealed that it was moonshine. I don't know if you want the details."

"No, not if it was nonsense. What an odd man your uncle is! What a difference there can be between brothers! So there is no news that deserves the name."

"Only that the threatened journey approaches, and must now be imminent. And that Audrey's education is complete.

She suggested it as an economy, and held to it afterwards. Miss Gibbon is to be general helpmate instead of governess."

"In other words is superfluous. A general helpmate is. She is a person who does what people could do for themselves."

"Well, with four women that may be a good deal," said the second son.

"Oh, it will not hurt her," said his mother.

"How hard women are to each other! Surely it will. A fourfold duty would hurt anyone."

"Does this house seem very small and humble to you after the other?" said Eliza to Malcolm.

"Yes, it does," he said, looking round. "And it is both."

"It is not. It is a pleasant, comfortable house, as you know very well. Do you think you could provide for a family like this, if you depended on yourself?"

"No, I do not. Neither now nor ever. I have been given no opportunity."

"Because we know of your prospects. Your brothers have to make their own way. You are at once more fortunate and less."

"I am more fortunate. And I recognise it. I would not change with them. I hope they are of those people who get more pleasure out of money, when they have earned it. I am not."

"I hope you show your uncle that you are grateful to him."

"Why should I do so? I am not grateful. He would alter the position if he could."

"You can do all you can to be of help to him."

"That is a good deal. And he is of very little help to me. He says he wishes Ursula was in my place. I often wish she was in his."

"Did your aunt send me any message?"

"No, I do not remember one."

"You could hardly have forgotten so soon. You have not been here for a week. She and I behave like strangers. No one would think we had married brothers."

"No one would assign you to the same species at all."

"Oh, and which species do you like the better?"

"Yours," said Malcolm, yielding to the unspoken compulsion and bending to her embrace.

"And which do you, Rudolf?"

"Yours."

"And you, Nigel?"

"Yours."

"My three dear boys!" said Eliza, caressing them in turn. "I am sure your aunt and uncle must envy me my sons. And they know that one of you must succeed them. I could feel for them there, if they would let me."

"The loss is yours," said Nigel.

"It is indeed," said Rudolf. "Feeling for people seems to satisfy all our needs. We look down on them and up to ourselves. And those are after all the chief ones."

"They would rather have their daughters than Mother's sons," said Malcolm. "They do not envy us. Make no mistake."

"I do not make one," said Eliza. "I am not a person who does so. They would have liked one of their children to be a son. They cannot expect us not to know it."

"I think they assume we do not. It is one of those things of which we are supposed to be unconscious."

"Well, I cannot be. How could I in my position? I am the wife of the younger son. I am left a widow. I have to live quite differently. It is natural to be aware of any advantage I have. I am a human woman."

"Perhaps Aunt Ellen is not," said Malcolm. "That would explain her."

"Oh, so you do like her better than your mother?"

"I daresay she is better. But I do not like her so well. I have a preference for human beings."

"Well, I am one of those. I have never thought I was anything else. Your father did not wish me to be. And your aunt has married one, whatever she is herself. Your uncle is human enough."

"Well, is he quite?" said Malcolm.

"He may be too human," said Nigel. "There ought to be something godlike in all of us."

"Perhaps there is in Uncle," said Rudolf. "He dares to be himself, even though daring is needed. And that is true of any gods we know."

"He has not much to hide," said Malcolm. "And so he does not trouble to hide it."

"I take trouble all the time," said Nigel.

"My life is one long, brave struggle," said Rudolf.

"Perhaps that explains the good accounts of you from Cambridge," said Eliza.

The mother and sons stood together; Malcolm taller than the others and looking somehow apart; Rudolf shorter and heavier, with large, grey eyes and a broad, plain, pleasant face; and Nigel slight and supple and more aware of himself, with straighter features and large, dark eyes, that gave him a claim to handsomeness. Eliza cared little for looks in men, and gave them no esteem for them, but demanded them in women and made much of her own. She was a short, fair, young-looking woman of fifty, with an almost beautiful, aquiline face, clear, grey, deep-set eyes, and lips and brows that were responsive to her emotions.

"Now I have a piece of news for you," she said, with her expression alert to mark any failure of interest. "You are to have a sister. You know I have lost an old friend, or I suppose you know. I have told you many times. Well, she has left me the guardian of an orphan daughter, who is coming to live with us for a while. Now what have you to say to it?"

"Nothing," said Rudolf. "I am afraid of not saying enough."

"Say some more yourself, Mother," said Nigel.

"You must not fall in love with her. You are too young, and she is not well off. You must just behave to her like brothers."

"I am already doing that to three people," said Malcolm. "I will leave this one to the others."

29

"I am awkward with women," said Rudolf. "Whether I fall in love with her or not, she will not with me."

"I feel I could not be awkward," said Nigel. "This may give me a chance to prove it."

"So your mother has not been enough for you," said Eliza. "You have wanted something more?"

"It is not our fault that we are to have it."

"Something is to be our fault," said Rudolf.

"Well, I will leave you to discuss it together. You must make the most of your elder brother, when he deigns to visit you."

"Uncle is not anxious for me to come and go," said Malcolm. "He likes me to belong to his house. And I see his reasons."

"You belong to his house, but not to him," said Eliza, with a flash of her eyes. "I am your mother and shall remain so. If he forgets, you must remind him."

"I was to show my gratitude to him. Is that the wisest way?"

"You are capable of more than one feeling," said Eliza, as she went to the door.

It opened almost as she closed it.

"So we are to have a change," said another voice.

"And you feel it is time, Mandy?" said Nigel.

"Well, we must all do that. It is time indeed. Things go on and on in the same way. And Malcolm's being in the other house has made no difference. He brings no news."

"I cannot make any," said the latter. "Things go on in the same way there as well."

"I suppose they do that in houses," said Rudolf. "Perhaps more than anywhere else. In every house things are going on in the same way. Think of rows of houses."

"Yes, life does not do much for people. And we cannot make it do any more."

"Only by our own effort," said Nigel. "And then it is not life that does it, but ourselves."

"Well, we must be ready for the change," said Miss

Manders, who was supposed to be Eliza's companion and was really her sons'. "I wonder what the girl will think of everything here."

"I do not," said Rudolf. "I know what she will think. What you and I do, Mandy. And what Nigel would, if he were prone to thought."

"We don't know what kind of life she has had."

"And so if she is prepared for this one. But do not be troubled. I expect she is. Most people would be. They have had that kind."

"I wonder what she will think of all of you," said Miss Manders, turning her long, thin face and large, kind eyes on them, in a way that showed her own opinion.

"Well, there is Nigel," said Rudolf. "But I hope we can explain about him. He is not all bad, poor boy."

"So this is how you talk to them, when I am not here!" said Eliza's voice. "I have suspected it for a long time, Miss Manders. And now I am sure. I ought never to leave them, unless you are out of the house. What a thing to have to say to someone I have trusted for years! I should have thought you would know better than to put them out of conceit with their home, when I give my life to managing it for them, in spite of my grief and loneliness. Oh, one woman should never trust another. I can trust no one. I am alone. I cannot even trust my sons to be loyal to me behind my back. But I thought you were one by yourself. I thought you were my friend."

"And so I am. And you know I am," said Miss Manders, in a tone of distress. "We were talking at random, and wondering if the guest would expect too much. You know how they do sometimes."

"No, I do not. And she may expect what she pleases in my house, as you know very well. You were belittling my children's home to them. I heard what you said and how you said it. You cannot escape from it now. I know what you are. I have suspected it and put it from me. Now I must accept it."

31

"You are born to be a figure in tragedy, Mother," said Nigel, "when you can be one on such a ground."

"I *am* a figure in tragedy, my dear. I was not born to be one. I was born for happiness and love and life. And they have been torn from me. You would think that people would extend to me a helping hand. But I am to have nothing; no kindness, no loyalty, no help in my hard place. I am a figure of tragedy indeed."

"You sustain the part well, if it is not natural to you," said Rudolf.

"Do I?" said Eliza, half-mollified. "Oh, there are many parts I could have filled, if I had had the chance, if I had had your opportunities. You don't know what is in your mother."

"We have had a fair illustration of it," said Malcolm.

"Have you? And what do you think of it?"

"Well, but poorly."

"Oh, you are not my son any longer. You are drifting away from your mother. You belong to the other house and the other life. You see her with a cold and critical eye. I suppose you are thinking how much better your aunt would have behaved in my place?"

"I was not doing so. But I do not doubt that she would."

"Let me tell you that she could not be in it. She has not lost her husband. She has not given up her eldest child. She has not had to struggle alone against odds too heavy for her. It is easy to be smooth and controlled, when there is nothing to contend with."

"Is that a description of Aunt Ellen's experience?"

"You know it is. I was foolish to make a comparison."

"Well, that does not usually have a happy result."

"What a dreary name 'Ellen' is! It reminds me of a great-grandmother."

"It might be the name of anyone. But it reminds me of my aunt."

"She is not your real aunt. Only one by marriage."

"Well, my uncle's being a real one does not help us."

"Is Malcolm staying to luncheon?" said Miss Manders, trying to use a normal tone.

"Yes, I am keeping him for it," said Eliza, putting the matter as she saw it. "I am entitled to his presence in my house. He does not return to me simply to rush away."

"Then I will tell them to lay another place."

"They will be equal to that without being told. It does not do to imagine we are achieving something. It is better to be honestly unoccupied, when we are."

Miss Manders remained in this state until they gathered at the table.

"So they have not been equal to laying my place," said Malcolm.

"Oh, I will do it in a moment," said Miss Manders, hastening to the sideboard.

"It is true that it will not take any longer," said Eliza, with a cold glance.

"Is your aunt expecting you for luncheon?" said Miss Manders to Malcolm, keeping her eyes on him.

"She may be, but such things do not seem to matter there."

"Then the house is badly managed," said his mother. "And there must be extravagance and waste."

"There is neither," said Malcolm.

"Oh, you are getting to feel competitive about it, and to make meaningless comparisons. You have soon become a member of the luxurious household. It has not taken you long."

"Well, it was what I had to do. And you urged me to it."

"But you need not lose all your feeling for your old home."

"And is this the way to make me keep it?"

"Surely I can say a word under my own roof without bringing this on my head."

"It depends on the word," said Malcolm. "You cannot say that one. I must fulfil my bargain with my uncle. It is the only honest thing. I ought not to be made to feel guilty over it."

"Surely you ought," said Nigel. "You will be richer and idler than we are."

"And as that gives us a sense of self-righteousness," said Rudolf, "it should give you one of guilt."

"Which life would you choose yourself?" said Eliza.

"My own," said Rudolf, meeting her eyes. "It gives me more personal scope and leaves me at home."

"My own dear boy! Which would you choose, Nigel?"

"As I have not the choice, it is not any good to make it."

"So you do feel half-envious of Malcolm?"

"That is what I feel. Half-envious, not wholly so."

"You soon feel the lure of the easier life."

"Well, everyone does that in a way."

"I should not have thought so. I do not. I only ask to have my dear ones about me, and reasonable comfort for myself and them. I should not be any happier for wealth and ease."

"You sometimes talk as if you would," said Malcolm.

"We are said not to be," said Nigel. "I do not know how far it is true. Rich people show no wish to become poorer."

"Malcolm is in a position to judge."

"No, I hardly am. The other household is a simple one. They would scarcely know what you mean by wealth and ease. Ease they have, of course. There is no sign of wealth. As far as I know, there is none."

"We may not be happier for wealth," said Nigel. "For ease and freedom we surely are."

"So you do envy Malcolm," said Eliza. "It had to come to that. I wonder if I was wise in letting him accept your uncle's offer."

"He must take his place in the end. There was no good in postponing it. It was best for him to learn to fill it."

"You would have found it an easy lesson?" said Eliza.

"Not many people would find it a hard one."

"I accepted the offer myself," said Malcolm. "It was no one else's doing."

"You would not have done so, if your mother had been against it."

"Yes, I believe I should."

"No, you would not. You would not have thought of it."

"I should simply have done it."

"You do not care for me as much as Rudolf does."

"No, naturally not. You have not cared for me as you have for him."

"But you do care for me?" said Eliza, on a startled note.

"Yes, I do."

"As much as you care for your aunt?"

"Yes, more than that. But perhaps hardly as much as I should have cared for her, if she had been my mother."

"Does she know how much you feel for her?"

"As matters are, I do not feel it. I have just told you."

"But you would have liked a mother of that kind?"

"Yes. So would most people."

"Would you, Rudolf?"

"No, I like my own mother."

"So Malcolm prefers someone who goes through life without much feeling."

"Is that a description of Aunt Ellen?" said Malcolm.

"Well, she does not appear to be much affected by things."

"She does not contrive an appearance out of scale with what is beneath."

"And is that a description of me?"

"Well, does the cap fit?" said her son.

"You have a different way of talking to me from the way Rudolf has."

"Well, perhaps you set me the example."

"I think the less people do for their children, the more they care for them!"

"The less they do of certain things perhaps."

"You mean I am too highly-strung, and have not your aunt's placid ways."

"No, that is what *you* mean."

"Well, you had better go back to her, and the house you like so much better than this one."

"Well, I shall have to go," said Malcolm, rising.

"I would not have believed it, Miss Manders," said Eliza, keeping her eyes from him. "That a few months in another house could alter anyone like this. He does not seem like my son. It is not much good to think and strive for someone for twenty-six years to lose him in a moment. It takes the meaning out of life. There seems to be nothing left. I feel I had better not have lived. I don't know what my husband would say to my being cast up high and dry like this, after braving the storm for so long."

"That is how Uncle talks of himself," said Malcolm, looking back. "If you have no affinity with my aunt, you might seek one with him."

"Father would think you could depend on yourself, Mother," said Nigel. "We know that he knew you could."

"He would not like me to be driven to doing so. How I sometimes long for an hour with him! Perhaps it is why I find it hard to bear with other people, that I am used to so much. But Malcolm would disappoint anyone. There is no good in glossing over the truth. You cannot flatter me into shutting my eyes to it. I am a person for looking truth straight in the face. Straight and full I look at it, undeterred by any threat it brings. That is the kind of mother you have. That is the kind of wife your father had. And it was the kind he was grateful for. None of you is up to his level, though Rudolf is the nearest to it."

"What is that?" said Miss Manders, hurrying to the window, her tone alert over any promise of change. "Someone is arriving! Someone is coming into the house! Malcolm is coming back with someone with him!"

This is what Malcolm was doing. He opened the door and ushered a girl into the room, following her in a protective manner, with his eyes on her face.

"Here is our guest, Mother, arrived betimes. Or, as she feels herself, too soon, driven by trains and tides and other forces. For us it is enough that she is with us."

"My dear!" said Eliza, hastening forward and taking the girl's hands, with her eyes on her face. "That is the chief thing indeed. But the trains and tides have done their work. You need to be at home, and you may feel this house is that.

Here are a mother and brothers for you. Here is Miss Manders to care for you. She is an expert at taking care of people. Poor child, you need the care."

The girl lifted her eyes to Eliza's, and the two alert, comely faces met each other. It seemed that something passed between them, and determined something further.

Verena Gray was of ordinary height and build, but of unusual and definite appearance. Her wide, blue eyes, thin mouth, straight features, high colour and strong chin seemed to give Eliza a clue to her, and the latter's eyes did not leave her as the talk went on.

"You are not like your mother. You are like no one I remember. You are like yourself. And that is what she would have chosen. She warned me not to look for a likeness, though 'warned' need not be the word. Well, now I have a daughter. And you will have—we will not say a mother, but someone who will try to do what she would wish for you."

"I have not thought of having brothers," said Verena, looking round. "I have often wished I had a sister."

"Well, there I cannot help you. You will have to be content with my boys, as other people are content with them. Malcolm hardly seems a boy to you. He is six years older than you are. And he has another home. His brothers are of your age, and will be with you. And when they are at Cambridge, you and I will make the best of each other. Or you will make the best of me, and I will be content with you as you are."

"Is this the best Mother can make of herself?" muttered Malcolm. "The worst seems always to be lurking underneath."

"I suppose it always is," said Nigel. "It is a question of how easily it rises to the surface."

"What are you whispering about?" said Eliza. "Verena must forgive you. A girl becomes a civilised creature earlier than a boy."

"I did not know that," said Malcolm. "It is not true of my cousins. But if it is of Verena, she and I should be on a

37

level. I am obliged to use her Christian name, as I know no other."

"Her names are Verena Eliza Gray. But I think you may use the first, as she will do the same."

"Now, has she had enough of new names and faces?" said Miss Manders, coming forward. "Should I not see her as my charge for the next hour?"

"Well, I will not introduce you," said Eliza. "It would make another name. And she may find the extra face enough."

"I shall find it so in two senses," said Verena, smiling as she followed.

"Well, what do you think of her?" said Eliza. "Are you glad to have the change? Or was your life enough for you?"

"Are the two things contradictory?" said Nigel.

"Yes, I think they are. What do you feel about having a sister?"

"As I have said, I am provided with them," said Malcolm. "But this will make an interest for all of us."

"What a lot of interest you need! I should have thought you had enough. Two homes and two families, and it seems two mothers. You are a change-loving person."

"Well, most of us want something besides our homes and families."

"That is how other homes and families come about," said Nigel.

"How a girl brings in another atmosphere!" said Eliza, looking from one to another. "Just a glimpse of one, and there is this difference! I had not thought of you as so much like other boys."

"Oh, pray do not think of us like that," said Rudolf. "Surely there is no need to go so far."

"Other boys!" said Nigel. "Mother should moderate her language."

"I suppose all mothers think their own sons are exceptional. But I somehow thought you were satisfied with what you had."

"Does acceptance of a new situation imply discontent with the old one?" said Rudolf.

"Well, it suggests that discontent would arise, if the first one returned. But this will not bring any real change for you. We have made a mistake in making so much of it. Your lives will remain as they are. It is I who will have to manage another. And I am used to arranging lives. I sometimes think it prevents me from giving enough attention to my own."

"Lives have a way of taking their own course," said Malcolm.

"So you have not gone back to your aunt," said Eliza. "Is there anything here that prevents you?"

"I was intercepted by the arrival. And now I have stayed so long, I may as well stay longer. Uncle likes me to be at his beck and call. He has no welcome for me, when I appear at my pleasure or at yours. You will have to learn that."

"I shall learn nothing. It is not for me to take lessons. You cannot teach your mother anything. And certainly your uncle cannot."

"He is already teaching you something. It is a new thing for you to remind me to return."

"The attraction here is new, isn't it?" said Eliza, more gently. "Well, wait for Verena, if that is what you want. I will go upstairs and let you have her to yourselves. You see you can depend on your mother."

"We are suspected of being ordinary in the average way," said Rudolf. "I was always afraid of Nigel's being found out. But it is shocking that suspicion should go further. Mother was certainly shocked."

"If we saw ourselves as ordinary, we should be less so than was possible," said Malcolm.

"Or so much so, that we were obliged to recognise it. We see that Mother was obliged to."

"She knows there is safety in numbers," said Nigel. "She takes the usual precautions."

"Ordinary qualities may be useful," said Malcolm. "I wish Mother had more of them."

"More of what?" said Eliza, returning to the room, as if there had been no word of her remaining away.

"Ordinary qualities," said Nigel.

"Oh, you think my qualities are not ordinary. Well, there may not be much that is ordinary about me. I do not see why there should be. Why, Miss Manders, you are soon at liberty. Is everything well upstairs?"

"Well, Verena is overtired. She will sleep for a while, and then come down. It is a change to have a girl to look after. I have always wished that one of the boys was a girl."

"I have not. I have never wanted them different."

"Oh, neither have I. I meant I should have liked a girl as well."

"That is not what you said," said Eliza. "Well, the arrival will be less of an event in the other house. There is no lack of girls there."

"They will be friends for Verena," said Malcolm. "She will not want to find a world peopled by males."

"I should not have minded at her age. I think it is what I almost found. And I do not remember that I found much fault with it."

"When she goes to the other house, she is to find a world peopled by Malcolm," murmured Rudolf.

"What did you say, my boy?" said Eliza.

Rudolf lightly repeated his words.

"Oh, you will all be brothers and sisters together. We are making too much of everything. There has been no great upheaval. Why, here is your new sister, ready to fulfil her part! Are you rested, my dear? I hear you have had a sleep."

"I slept for a time. My head was too full for me to sleep much. My whole world seems in confusion."

"Yes, I hardly think I could have slept at all. I should have been too shaken and wrought-up. I am glad you have not such an awkward temperament."

"It is true that it has had its awkwardness," said Malcolm.

"Oh, it is the highest type, you know," said Eliza. "But it

is not so easy for the person who has it. So I am glad if Verena has escaped it."

"But has she? I should have said your adjectives might fit her."

"Would you? She looks very nice and fresh. More so than I think she could, if that were the case. What does she say herself?"

"Oh, I must belong to the higher type. I could not be attached to any other," said Verena, in a light tone, but with changing eyes. "I will claim my place from the first."

"Ought you not to be going, my boy?" said Eliza to Malcolm, as if she had not heard.

"Yes, I ought. I do not live here, Verena. I have been received into my uncle's house to impersonate the son they should have had. My character is that of substitute and second-best."

"And Verena takes the place of the daughter I should have had," said Eliza, caressing the latter's cheek. "So the lack in both households has been filled."

"Did you want a daughter?" said Verena, looking into her face. "I can only imagine you with sons."

"Yes, many people have said that. And all my life I have had to do with men. And I was glad that my children were boys. But it is a good thing to miss nothing."

"You are not like my father," said Malcolm. "I remember he wanted a girl."

"There is someone whom you are not like to-day, my boy, and that is yourself. It is your habit to be taciturn. What has unloosed your tongue?"

"Perhaps it is Verena's arrival and seeing you with a daughter. As she said, it was hard to imagine it."

"Well, you do not need to. It has become the fact. And her mother trusted her to me. So she had more imagination. Oh, I have been called upon to fulfil many parts."

"I have been called upon to fulfil one," said Rudolf.

"And you have fulfilled it, my boy," said Eliza, stroking his shoulder. "And he does much, who does a little well."

"How untrue that is!" said Malcolm. "He who does much, has usually attempted more, and often sacrificed himself to it."

> " 'This high man, with a great thing to pursue,
>   Dies ere he knows it.' "

quoted Verena.

"So you sum up the matter," said Eliza. "Or rather the poet does. I see that my niece, Constance, will have a competitor."

"It is I who will have that," said Malcolm. "I pursue the great thing of being a son to Uncle. And Verena will do the corresponding thing here. We play parallel parts."

"Well, opposite ones," said Eliza.

CHAPTER IV

"WHY, ELIZA!" SAID Miles. "Why, I am glad to see you.
But you know we are just about to leave?"

"Yes, that is why I am here. We have come to say our
farewell. To wait for a message was to wait in vain, and we
could only take matters into our own hands. You will say a
word to your nephews before you leave them? You may not
see me as a relation, and I am not one by blood. But they are
your brother's sons, and have a claim on your affection. Or do
you not feel it?"

"Why, Eliza, of course I do. They are like my younger
sons, as Malcolm is like my eldest. And indeed I see you as a
relation, when you are my brother's wife. How else could I
see you? But I have been so harassed in these last days. I
have hardly said a word to my nearest and dearest, from whom
I am about to part. And the moment has come when I must
do so. Goodbye, my daughters. Farewell, my three most dear
ones. May you fare well indeed. It goes to my heart to leave
you. I feel I am leaving the heart behind, and I put a part of
it in your keeping. And I am taking your mother from you.
I could not face the exile alone. I need her support in the
trials that lie ahead. I do not hesitate to own my dependence
on her. When a woman has help to give her husband, he
should be the first to recognise it. Who can know it as well as
he? He should be proud that it is so. That is my reason for
taking her, and I could not have a better. You can feel that
your father and mother are working together for your good."

"I wonder if I should have liked my husband to talk about
me in that way," said Eliza to her sons.

"I should like anyone to do so about me," said Rudolf.

"We know you are doing it for the best, Father," said
Constance. "There is no need to tell us."

43

"Does she mean that that speech is wasted?" said Rudolf. "It made tears start to my eyes."

"I am simply suggesting that our feeling confirms it," said his cousin.

"My Audrey, you are crying," said Miles, more loudly. "My brave girls were speeding me with dry eyes, but yours have overflowed. Your father will remember your tears, as his distance widens. In a sense he will carry them with him."

"I wish he had noticed mine," said Rudolf. "When a man's tears are so pathetic."

"I hope this scene will not be prolonged," said Ursula. "It must weaken as it continues."

"It will mean what it does, whatever its length," said Constance.

"She does not know that she is saying the same thing," said Malcolm.

"Miss Gibbon, I leave you in charge," said Miles. "You and my nephew will watch over them. And you will have my gratitude when I return, as return I shall, please God."

"I was wrong," said Ursula. "The scene is gathering force."

"It is simply taking its natural course," said Constance.

"Well, the power of Nature is great," said Nigel.

"A voyage is no longer dangerous," said Malcolm. "There is no need to doubt the return and Miss Gibbon's reward."

"And a reward of the most valuable kind," said Constance.

"Is Nature misusing her power?" said Rudolf.

"Mother," said Constance, in a lower tone, "Aunt Eliza suggests that they shall all join us this evening, to help us to end the day. I think she really feels it will help us. So perhaps we should accept the offer."

"Well, I am glad of it," said Miles. "I am glad to think there will be no sad faces on your first night alone. I am not a person who wants to leave tears behind. Though if my Audrey finds it hard to help them, she can feel there is an especial bond between her and her father."

"So it is what he does want," said Nigel.

"It is not a necessary inference," said Constance.

"Eliza, it is kind of you to be here," said Ellen. "It supports us through the parting scene. We had it last night to avoid it to-day, but it did not even serve as a rehearsal. This one bears no likeness to it."

"Mrs. Mowbray, I will not say much," said Miss Gibbon. "But you may rely on me to fulfil my charge."

"And that is saying it all, Miss Gibbon," said Miles. "No further word could enhance it."

"Everyone is perfect," said Ellen. "We can detect no flaw anywhere. Let us go before any human weakness emerges. I don't know what Eliza can say to so much perfection. She may not be prepared for it."

"She is supplying her own," said Malcolm. "And has brought some in Rudolf, and is prepared for both. In Nigel and me she brings the human weakness, and is also prepared for it."

"You are wrong," said Eliza, coldly. "I was not prepared for so much."

"Come, my love," said Miles. "The farewell scene will remain with us. To prolong it is to add nothing."

"I thought it was adding a good deal," said Nigel.

"And I admired every addition," said Rudolf. "Words are so much more difficult than silence."

"The easier course may be the safer," said Malcolm. "It is a mistake to aim too high."

"Malcolm is not at his best," said Eliza. "He is too much away from his home."

"We shall have the scene to carry with us," said Constance. "I would not be without the memory."

"I think I would," said Ursula.

"And I am sure I would," said Audrey.

"We know Audrey has tried to be brave," said Miss Gibbon.

Constance gave a long, grave look at her sister.

"I shall cry if I like," said the latter, in a defiant tone.

"It was Uncle who liked it," said Nigel. "She can feel she did what she could for him at the last."

"We all did that in different ways," said Constance. "And now we can do the next thing for him. He would wish us to cheer up and settle down. And we must bring ourselves to it. Aunt Eliza and the boys will support us to-night."

"Is their guest coming with them?" said Miss Gibbon. "That would give a festive air to things."

"That is hardly what we want perhaps."

"It is not what we shall have," said Malcolm.

"Well, I am not so sure," said Eliza. "We do not want long faces. And we shall not be doing our part, if we have them. That is not what their parents would ask of us. Yes, our guest is coming, if I may bring her. And if her presence does what Miss Gibbon suggests, we will find no fault with it. We need hardly say goodbye, as we are to reappear."

"I am sure Aunt Eliza is good at heart," said Constance, looking after them.

"That is a hard thing to say," said Ursula.

"You know it was not meant to be. We do not forget that we are speaking of Malcolm's mother."

"Ursula was not sure," said Malcolm.

"How I should like to meet someone who was bad at heart!" said Audrey. "It would be such a pleasant person."

"We shall not help matters by sneering at each other," said Constance. "How should we feel, if Father and Mother were listening?"

"I feel it is rather a pity they are not."

"I think I will go upstairs for a time. Perhaps the fewer of us down here, the better. We shall be saying things we may regret."

"You should regret that," said Malcolm. "There was no reason for it."

Constance went to the door, and in a moment turned back.

"I do regret it, if I ought," she said.

"Well, ought you or not? That is the question."

Constance stood silent.

"Let us have an end of this," said Ursula. "We are making a scene out of nothing."

"Well, a scene will clear the air sometimes," said Miss Gibbon.

"It can do the opposite," said Malcolm. "I speak of what I know."

"I do regret saying what I did," said Constance, and went quickly from the room.

There was a pause.

"Is Constance preparing her way to eternity?" said Malcolm.

"It is an embarrassing process," said Ursula. "And she is only doing something for herself. One sees why that is not approved."

"It cannot meet much credit in family life."

"Oh, the girls are the best of friends," said Miss Gibbon.

"Well, we may not want our best friends to have much credit," said Ursula.

"My mother is the person who has that, or takes it," said Malcolm.

"Well, I am sure she deserves a great deal," said Miss Gibbon.

"In what way?" said Eliza's son.

"Well, she is a widow, and has brought up three boys. She has had great responsibilities."

"Why is that to her credit? I see it may deserve compassion."

"Well, she has managed it so successfully."

"And to command success is always a credit," said Ursula. "So much so, that people say it is more to deserve it. That shows how hard it is to get it. They have to soften the alternative."

"To command it you would have to deserve it so much," said Audrey. "And then you might be too sensitive to be so overbearing. That may be doing more and deserving it. I suppose it is."

"My mother has commanded many things," said Malcolm. "But she has not always been obeyed."

"She certainly has a commanding personality," said Miss Gibbon.

Constance returned to the room with a composed expression.

"I believe Constance has conquered herself," murmured Audrey.

"Come, do not whisper," said Miss Gibbon.

"What is the secret?" said Constance, pleasantly.

"Something to do with you," said Malcolm.

"Then it can be said aloud. I do not want anything to do with me to be whispered."

"You would want this to be."

"No, you are mistaken."

"Well, would you like to take the risk?"

"There is none," said Constance.

"Well, we said you had conquered yourself."

There was a pause.

"Well, that is nothing to be ashamed of," said Constance, easily.

"Oh, surely you are ashamed of it."

"Would you be?"

"I should be ashamed of making the effort."

"We all have to do it sometimes."

"Constance has really conquered herself," said Ursula to Malcolm. "And though she is not ashamed of herself, we are ashamed of her. And I believe she is rather ashamed."

"Now I think we all ought to look to-night as Mother would wish," said Constance, in a tone of wisely broaching another subject. "And I suggest that we repair to our rooms in time to do so."

"There is nothing against it," said Ursula. "But why should we want to appear to disadvantage?"

"Well, we must not let the occasion make us careless or indifferent. We know how Mother liked us to look, and we owe it to her to remember it."

"We owe it to ourselves, which is a safer incentive."

"It is not in my case."

"Well, the result will be the same."

"It may be to the outward eye," said Constance.

"Well, appearance is directed to that."

"You do not quite understand what I mean."

"Yes I do, and I am with you. But I think that Mother's wishes and ours will coincide."

"Well, I am glad if they do," said Constance.

"Constance is conquering herself again," murmured Audrey. "She should soon be mistress of herself, with nothing more to be done."

Constance's advice was followed, and Eliza's eyes marked the result and showed that they did so.

"So you have cheered up after the farewell scene. I did not know it was to be a festive evening. But I am glad you have recovered your spirits enough to make it so."

"We did not want to show any signs of depression," said Constance.

"Well, you do not indeed, though I think they would be excusable. Why, it might be the day of reunion rather than the opposite."

"So it might," said Ursula. "We shall wear the same dresses."

"So you make no difference between the two occasions."

"Well, with small wardrobes no difference is made between a good many occasions."

"Why, I am sure I know dresses of yours less festive than these."

"No doubt you do. You know all our dresses. But the others are so much less festive."

" 'Festive' seems rather an unexpected word," said Constance.

"Yes," said Eliza, looking from one to another. "Yes, perhaps it does."

"They are doing you honour, Mother," said Nigel, "the more, if they are forgetting other things to do it."

"But I do not feel I am doing it to them. And I should not

49

have asked for forgetfulness. I do not feel I am gracing the occasion."

"Let us forget the question of our appearance," said Constance. "We have other things to remember."

"Why, you have certainly not done the first," said Eliza, laughing. "There is every sign of attention to it."

"I thought that was supposed to be the way to forget it," said Rudolf.

"Pray let us find some way," said Malcolm.

"I hardly think we are supposed to do that," said Eliza, looking at her nieces. "And you ought not to want to forget your mother's appearance, when justice has not been done to it. It ought to be a matter of concern to you."

"It is not a matter of general concern."

"No, I see it is not. And I cannot be accused of expecting it to be. I have given it so much less attention than other people."

"But now you are giving it much more."

"Oh, I do not know. I detect signs of complacence," said Eliza, looking round and smiling. "It makes me wish that I had taken more thought for Verena. I feel I am failing both her mother and myself."

"Then you see how we felt, when we tried to look as Mother would have wished," said Constance, at once.

Eliza smiled at the feeling displayed.

"All black dresses look much the same," said Rudolf.

"Now that is a man's speech," said Miss Gibbon. "You might as well say that all purple dresses look the same."

"Well, they are more the same than those of different colours. They have purpleness in common."

"I am sure the right thing to say is that difference shows the most in black," said Nigel.

"There is something in it," said Miss Gibbon.

"Men know nothing about women's clothes," said Malcolm. "Women dress for each other."

"I wish we had not dressed for Aunt Eliza," murmured Audrey.

"Why," said Malcolm, "when the success is so great?"

"Shall we not change the subject?" said Constance.

"Why, when it is so near to your hearts?" said Eliza, kindly. "And I congratulate you on the result."

"They can hardly congratulate you on it," said Malcolm.

"Mother has given them the truest congratulation," said Nigel.

"Yes, I have shown a sense of inferiority. You see I knew what was wanted. There are things that women know about each other."

"Shall we now talk about the men's clothes?" said Nigel.

"There is not the same scope for difference," said Miss Gibbon.

"Now surely that is a woman's speech."

"I hope it is a true one," said Ursula. "We do not want it all a second time."

"I do. I long for it," said Nigel.

"I wonder what your mother is wearing to-night," said Eliza, to her nieces.

"I will wonder what Uncle is wearing," said her son.

"I hope not dressing-gowns," said Ursula. "They will both be seasick."

"Oh, it is too soon for that," said Eliza. "How have you pictured your mother, Constance?"

"I had not pictured her in anything particular."

"What a confession!" said Malcolm.

"Well, they had enough to think of in that line at home," said Eliza.

"How do you picture her, Mother?"

"As the most impressive figure on the boat, whatever she is wearing."

"That is no answer. I expect Constance thinks of her in that way."

"I expect so too," said Eliza, with cordiality. "Do you not, Constance?"

"I had not exactly thought about it."

51

"Well, your indifference has had its result. I thought about it too much to remember myself. And I ought to have remembered Verena."

"I must say it again, Aunt Eliza. It was our thought of Mother, that made us want to appear as she would have liked."

"And I am sure she thinks of you as doing so, and is proud of her successful daughters."

"Mother, what would she think of you?" said Malcolm.

"I do not feel that anyone thinks much about me in these days, my son."

"How do you manage in your new life?" said Ursula, in a low tone to Verena. "It must make its claim."

"It does not make one like this. Your aunt is different at home. But I am afraid of her. I feel it might be made."

"You have now had light thrown on her," said Malcolm. "Have you the courage to face it?"

"No, I shall shut my eyes to it. I think she half-expects that of people. She almost has a right to. She has trained them to accept her as she is."

"What are you laughing at, Malcolm?" said Eliza. "Very few people can make you do that. Will you not share the jest?"

"No, that request is never followed."

"Not when your mother makes it?"

"No, it would cease to be a jest. Indeed it has already done so."

"You look pale, Audrey, my dear," said Eliza, turning from her son.

"She does," said Constance. "She has found the day too much."

"Well, I expect she has. I think the rest of you have sustained it beyond praise. Well, she must think of her mother as triumphant and admired on the high seas."

"She is thinking of herself as neither, in a bereft home," said Ursula.

"Poor, little, orphan girl!" said Eliza, putting her hand on

Audrey's shoulder. "That is how my boys would feel, if I had to leave them. I should not expect anything else. In a way I should hardly want it."

"Audrey has done her best with the day," said Miss Gibbon. "I have been proud of them all."

"And I think this is the niece of whom I am proudest," said Eliza, still caressing Audrey. "Or perhaps I should say with whom I am most in sympathy."

"You came here to keep up their spirits," said Malcolm. "Why did you do so, if you were out of tune with the object?"

"I found the object already attained, my boy. And I was a thought taken aback. It is true that I was."

"It is time to go into dinner," said Constance. "And I think we seem to need a break."

"That is the sort of need that is not generally stated," said Eliza, laughing. "But it is in keeping with the general good spirits."

"Verena, will you sit by Malcolm?" said Ursula.

"He would like his mother to be next to him," said Eliza. "We are not used to being separated."

"Well, you can sit on his left side."

"Can I?" said Eliza, laughing again. "What an odd way of putting it! And it will lead to his attention's being distracted from the right."

"Verena is the guest, Aunt Eliza. You are a relation."

"Yes, I know that, my dear. That is why I am here. I am so near a relation that ordinary conventions hardly count."

"Does it matter to you on which side of him you sit?"

"Ursula, my child, you need your mother with you."

"Of course I do. That is the meaning of this gathering."

"Well, I think I must try to take her place. I will sit on one side of Malcolm, as you would put it. And Miss Gibbon will sit on the other. She is not a relation, and is older than the rest of you. Verena will sit with the younger ones, as she would wish. It is her natural place."

"Her natural place is here," said Malcolm, drawing out a

chair by his own. "You must do as you please, Mother. I do not pretend to follow you."

"I think you should pretend to, my boy, if you really do not. You owe something to your mother."

"Surely not that, when you always recommend the truth."

"Well, I will sit in quite a different place," said Eliza, in a lighter tone, moving down the table. "I will sit between Rudolf and Audrey, my especial son and niece. That will suit us all and will take no account of convention. It is a senseless thing amongst members of a family."

"Well, we are all sitting somewhere," said Constance, taking her own seat.

"No one would contradict that. But it is hardly a thing to be said. I am in your mother's place, and I am going to tell you so."

"Who put you in that place?" said Malcolm.

"The fitness of things, my boy."

"I should have thought Ursula was in it."

"Well, think again, my dear."

"Mrs. Mowbray," said Miss Gibbon, smiling, "I am going to say an arrogant thing. In a sense I am in that place myself. My age and my length of time with my pupils were seen as fitting me for it. But of course that does not count when you are here."

"No, of course not. And to-night I am here. So nothing further need trouble us. And you must be glad not to come out of your chosen sphere."

"I should think it will be some time before she is here again," said Malcolm to Verena.

"What did you say, my boy?" said Eliza.

"I said it to Verena."

"Well, now you will say it to me. You heard me ask you what you said?"

"And I told you to whom I said it."

"Malcolm, something is altering you very much."

"Perhaps something is, just as the same thing once altered you."

"What do you mean, my son?"

"People never ask that, unless they know the answer."

"I think you must give it to me."

"As I have said, there is no need."

Eliza waited for a moment, controlling all her features but her eyes.

"Well, well, my boy, so your mother is to say it for you. You have come on a new experience. And its newness is enhancing it. You are taking your steps on a fresh road, and do not know that they may have to be retraced. Go on taking them. They may stand you in their stead. There is no need to answer. Your mother understands."

"That is the last thing you do, if you are being sincere."

"You think no one can do so? Of course you must think it. The fuller the understanding, the more it seems to you a lack of it. You have a right to sympathy and forbearance. Do I not carry the table with me?"

"You do indeed," said Ursula. "And we are grateful to be saved from making a speech."

"We all hope they will both be very happy," said Constance.

"So Constance was not saved from it," said Nigel.

"I should like so much to make one," said Rudolf. "Parts of it keep occurring to me. The best parts."

"Did Father and Mother know, before they went away?" said Audrey.

"No," said Malcolm. "They will know when they come back. Indeed before that, as letters are to reach them."

"Yes, that is the pity of it," said Eliza. "That it has come to pass without their sanction. But of course it has not done so. You will wait for it, and I daresay welcome the pause."

"It seems strange that it should happen on the day of their going," said Constance.

"Yes, that thought was mine. But perhaps it is not strange. It may be that the emotions of the day brought it into being, gave it the impetus it needed."

"It was already in being," said Malcolm.

"Father and Mother have not even met Verena," said Audrey.

"No," said Eliza. "It is one of the sudden things, a chance step into fairyland. But if it steadies, that is easily remedied."

"Will Malcolm and Verena live here, when they are married?"

"Oh, leave them in fairyland for the present. You want to bring the tale to its close. Let it go on in its reasonless, fairy way. And destiny cannot fulfil itself without its arbiters."

"Did you not manage your own romance?" said Verena, not looking at Eliza.

"My romance! It was one by itself. I have not met another like it."

"I suppose we all feel that about our own."

"Do you?" said Eliza, with a faint smile. "No, there is such a difference."

"It must always be the old, old story," said Constance, with a touch of emotion. "And of course a new one as well."

"Did not the romance lead to your marriage?" said Verena, now meeting Eliza's eyes. "It did not give place to others?"

"Not in my case, no. It led to marriage and a life of fulfilment. But a man makes essays and trials that lead him to the real thing, and mark the difference when it comes. Those had played their part, and I felt tenderly towards them. I feel tenderly now."

"There is not always that difference between men and women," said Malcolm. "Some women have something that you had not."

"And I had something that other women have not. Do you not remember it, my son?"

Malcolm did not reply.

"Do you remember it, Rudolf?"

"Yes, I do."

"Do you, Nigel?"

"I remember what you mean. I do not know if other women ever have it."

"I wonder what your father and mother are doing now,"

said Eliza, turning from them to the sisters. "Have you any idea?"

"No," said Ursula. "I had forgotten them for the moment."

"That is not what you mean," said Constance. "We have not forgotten people, because we do not happen to be thinking of them."

"So you are not thinking of them either?" said Eliza, smiling. "Is my Audrey giving them a thought?"

"I was thinking of Malcolm and Verena."

"And that put the nearer people out of your mind," said Eliza, in a tone of understanding. "I seem to be the person whose thoughts follow them. Perhaps more than theirs often follow me."

"Mother, do you feel you are at your best to-night?" said Malcolm.

"No, my dear. This hint of an engagement has brought my own back to me, and torn up the past and shown me the present in its emptiness. I can hardly be expected to be at my best."

"Shall we go to the drawing-room?" said Ursula. "There is more wine on the sideboard, if anyone wants it."

"The boys will not stay behind," said Eliza. "They do not need more wine. They are better without it."

"Is that their view?" said her niece.

"It is their mother's, and so theirs."

Malcolm rose and walked towards the door with Verena, as if the decision suited him.

"Now men do not go out of the room before women," said Eliza, half-laughing. "And very young women wait for older ones. It comes of living in the fairy-tale."

Malcolm drew back, waited for the line to pass, and caught up Verena, as though it made little difference.

"Dear me, this is not a very successful evening," said Constance, as they followed their aunt. "And the guests were supposed to enliven it."

"What did you say, my dear?" said Eliza, looking back.

"Oh, just something to Ursula."

57

"Then it is to me as well. What is said to anyone, is said to everyone, you know, on an occasion like this."

"I am afraid this was said just to Ursula."

"I am afraid it was," said Eliza, gravely. "And, you know, it should not have been."

"And it need not have been," said Ursula, impatiently. "Constance only said it was not a successful evening."

"Well, it could not be, could it, with your parents gone? Though I have thought it was more so to you than it might have been. And I have recognised your courage amongst the other qualities. For me it has been a strange evening, with its stirring up of the past, and its foreshadowing of things that may even touch the future. It has almost seemed incongruous on the day of parting. But it was a brave thought to have the evening, and a kind one to ask us to it."

"It has taken more kindness than they bargained for," said Malcolm.

"Yes, it has, my dear. A demand has been made on them. Though I did not know we made a bargain. I did not feel myself a party to one."

"Well, let us ask no more of them."

"No, let us not. Try to come out of yourself and be of some help to them."

"You forget that I live with them," said Malcolm.

"No, I do not. I should hardly forget it, when it means that you no longer live with me. I must be alive to the difference."

"God knows how I ever did that," muttered Malcolm.

"What does God know?" said his mother.

"Everything according to you. So there is no need to specify one thing."

"Then why did you do so?"

Malcolm turned away, and Eliza moved to Rudolf and put her hand on his shoulder.

"This is the son who could never say a rough word to his mother."

"I claim to be his equal in that respect," said Nigel.

"My two dear boys!" said Eliza, drawing them together. "How I have depended on you! How we depend on each other!"

"You have depended on Malcolm as much and more," said Verena. "Or you would not suffer from the loss of him."

"Yes, he has been my equal, companion son. And he will be so again. He has only gone a little apart. The steps can be retraced. And such steps leave no footprints."

"All experience must leave its marks," said Constance.

"Yes, I think I should have said so," said Miss Gibbon.

"No, not all," said Eliza, in a quiet tone.

"It is a pity Aunt Eliza has such a transparent mind," said Audrey to Ursula. "It is embarrassing to see into it all the time."

"Very few minds invite inspection."

"But most of them are not laid open to it."

"What are they saying about me?" said their aunt.

"That you have a transparent mind," said Malcolm.

"Yes, I have nothing to hide. And so I hide nothing," said Eliza, with the light in her eyes. "Nothing lurks and cowers in my thought. If it did, I would pluck it out and cast it from me. If you do not want truth, it is no good to come to me."

"We do not want it, or more of it, as you reveal it to us. It would be much better hidden."

"Oh, I know people draw a veil over themselves. But I am not so like everyone else."

"You really have an exaggerated likeness to them."

"Do you mean that I go further than they do?"

"Well, you can put it in that way."

"I am content to be on a level with other people," said Constance.

"That may show that you are not entirely on their level," said Miss Gibbon, kindly.

"How seldom people make a pretty speech!" said Eliza. "And how pleasant it is to hear it, when they do!"

"I think Father is ready to make them," said Constance.

"Yes, to his family. And I am going to do the same. It is a

good example to follow. I congratulate my nieces on the pleasure they have given us. The hours have slipped by unawares. We will not say farewell, as we shall soon forgather. And we found a happier thing to say. Come, Verena. Come, my sons. Goodbye, my other dear ones. We shall have such a pleasant memory."

"We must try not to have a memory at all," said Malcolm, as he returned from the hall.

"That is hardly in our power," said Constance.

"Aunt Eliza must think it is," said Ursula. "She can scarcely be explained in any other way."

"Is she a happy woman?" said Audrey.

"No one who thinks she is a goddess, can be happy," said Malcolm. "She must be always finding that people do not agree."

"In a way I have always agreed," said Ursula. "I grant her superhuman qualities. Her self-esteem and insistence on support for it are above the human scale."

"Well, gods do have to be given open praise," said Audrey.

"We know better than to talk like this," said Constance.

"No one can know how to talk about Aunt Eliza. And why does she not want Malcolm and Verena to marry?"

"She is jealous of his marrying at all," said Ursula. "And she thinks he should make a better match."

"He is her eldest son," said Constance. "And he is Father's heir. We may as well say the whole truth."

"I should not like to be Miss Manders," said Audrey.

"Now I think that is a forgivable speech," said Miss Gibbon. "I admit that I feel the same."

"Perhaps she has hardly the qualities to enable her to choose her posts," said Constance.

"No, perhaps not, Constance. Indeed definitely not. Though it was not what I meant to imply."

"Will Malcolm and Verena live in this house, when they are married?" said Audrey, for the second time.

"That cannot be decided until Father comes home," said Constance.

"It is decided already," said Malcolm. "We shall live in a separate one."

"That is for Father to say."

"It is for me, and I have said."

"You know you cannot say it on your own authority."

"I have done so," said her cousin.

"But you know the words mean nothing."

"They mean what they say."

"No words have meaning, unless they are related to truth."

"These are more than related. They are true."

"Father will settle that question and many others."

"He will hear the answers to them."

"Which of you will have the sense to stop?" said Ursula.

"Now, Constance, I think we may ask it of you," said Miss Gibbon.

"I am quite willing to change the subject."

"I am not," said Malcolm. "I am willing to drop it. I will discuss no subject with you."

"I did not mean to annoy you."

"You knew you were saying what would do so."

Constance paused for introspection.

"I can honestly say that I did not mean to annoy you, when we began to speak."

"A good many disputes come about in that way."

"I should not call this a dispute."

"Come, do not begin another," said Miss Gibbon.

"I wonder what those boys are saying to their mother," said Ursula. "I should like to listen to them. They can hardly walk home in silence."

This is what Rudolf and Nigel did, until Eliza spoke.

"Well, have you nothing to say about the evening?"

"Ursula managed well," said Rudolf. "It was rather a complex occasion."

"It did not present any especial problem. Unless they thought I made one with my open speaking."

"They thought you did, and they were right. And I doubt if they regarded the speech as open."

"If they were deaf to your innuendoes, what would be the good of them?" said Nigel.

"Oh, so you thought I made myself felt," said Eliza.

"I was sure you did. I wished I could be in doubt."

"And you thought I did it well?"

"Yes, but I could not see it as worth doing."

"But they liked having me?" said Eliza, with a note of anxiety.

"What do you really think?" said Rudolf.

"I am a more unusual person than they are used to having."

"That is true. But the advantage of unusualness depends on the form it takes."

"They did not always see the meaning of what I said."

"I always saw it," said Verena, in a quiet tone.

"No, not the whole," said Eliza. "Neither you nor they."

"Malcolm saw the whole. And he will remember it."

"Yes, of course. It was meant for him. He and I understand each other."

"You do not understand him."

"No, of course I do not, as you see it now," said Eliza, turning to her kindly. "You have your own picture of him. It is one that will shift and change like an autumn sky. Mine might be graven on stone."

Nothing more was said until they reached the house. Then Eliza and Verena went upstairs, and the brothers awaited Miss Manders.

"Mandy, there is news again," said Nigel. "Malcolm and Verena are going to be married."

"Oh, it has come out, has it?"

"Yes. Did you know? Did they tell you?"

"No, but of course I saw it."

"Of course you did," said Rudolf. "And we were taken by surprise. Can it be that we are yet unversed in life?"

"Well, how was it taken?"

"In a way that will remain with us."

"Yes," said Miss Manders, nodding. "I had better go upstairs to Verena."

"Nigel, we have suffered to-night," said Rudolf. "And more for others than for ourselves. I found myself forgetting myself. And I thought that was really never done."

"Are we too sensitive for this world?"

"No, but for this family."

"You cannot use a more particular word?"

"No, I cannot," said Rudolf.

CHAPTER V

"My dears, what can I say? How shall I tell you?" said Miss Gibbon. "It is too much to ask of anyone. It is too hard a thing to do."

"It is half-done," said Malcolm. "You can tell the whole."

"Say it," said Constance. "Anything is better than suspense."

Audrey drew back, as though this might not be.

"It can hardly mean more to you than it does to me."

"So it is Mother!" said Ursula. "Tell us the whole truth."

"Yes, your father will return to you, and your mother will not. The telegram was sent to me, to spare you the shock. But nothing can spare it or help you. It must be what it is."

"It is worse than suspense," said Audrey, turning away.

"Yes," said Malcolm. "Suspense has something of hope."

"Who sent the telegram?" said Irsula.

"Someone who was dealing with the troubles of the sunk ship. Your father had given my name in case of need. It tells the bare truth, and a letter is to follow. But it can tell little more. Little more seems to be known."

"Why should Miss Gibbon have the shock?" said Audrey, in an empty tone.

"So anything may rise up before us!" said Constance.

"We need not say it," said Malcolm. "We must find the thought enough."

"It is better to voice it. Silence cannot alter the truth."

"Neither can anything else alter it," said Audrey.

"We shall have to think how to help Father to face it."

"It will be enough to do so ourselves," said Ursula.

"To help him will be to help ourselves the most."

"There is no help," said Audrey. "What can change it for

him or us? All our lives before us, and Father with us by himself!"

"That is the thought that must be with us. That is the conclusion of everything. That is what we must remember."

"Is it likely we should forget?"

"This will mean more to Ursula and Audrey—to some of us than to Uncle," said Malcolm.

"You know that can hardly be true," said Constance.

"To me it seems that it is."

"Well, we will not differ to-day. But Mother is—Mother was Father's wife, and is—and was more to him than anyone else can be."

"Yes, it is a sad state of things," said Malcolm, in a tone of sympathy.

Constance turned away.

"Do not try not to cry, my dears," said Miss Gibbon.

"We are not trying," said Ursula, "or I am not. There is no need."

"You will come to it soon, and find that things are easier."

"They will be the same. But we ourselves may be so."

"That does not matter. If only I could help you!"

"And help yourself," said Malcolm. "I wish you could."

"It is Father who will have the first claim on us," said Constance. "We cannot say it too often."

Malcolm was about to speak, but checked the words.

"He will feel that himself," said Ursula. "How should he not?"

"Yes, we see part of the future," said her cousin.

"I cannot look at it yet," said Constance. "And he must fill the way."

"I wish something could," said Audrey. "There is nothing there."

"Well, we will let him do so. Then we shall have one feeling and one aim. And I think this may do one thing for us. It may draw us closer."

"That will not count amongst the other things."

"I have no aim," said Ursula. "I almost have no feeling."

65

"I have none of either," said Audrey. "I never shall have again."

"I do not see that bitterness will help us," said Constance. "And it will make us a strain on each other."

"Malcolm, you must help me to help them," said Miss Gibbon.

"You and I need help ourselves. That means there is none."

"Mrs. Malcolm Mowbray!" said Everard at the door.

"Yes, I sent the message to your aunt," said Miss Gibbon. "I sent it before I told you. I thought she might do it for me. But I remembered your father had given my name, and did it myself."

"Yes, we belong to you more than to her," said Ursula.

"My poor ones! My dear ones!" said Eliza's voice. "What can I say to you? What can I do? If only I could do something! All my life I will do what I can. But it will be so little. And your need is so great. What change a day can bring to us! I have myself faced the greatest change."

A faint smile crept to Malcolm's face.

"It is kind of you to come, Aunt Eliza," said Constance.

"It is kind of you to see me. It is kind to let me do anything. I shall be grateful for the kindness. I am here to beg it of you. And you will command my sons to any service. They wait upon your word."

"Malcolm is being very good to us," said Ursula.

"My poor boy, this is your grief as well. If I have ever resented your feeling for your aunt, I am glad of it now. How could you have felt too much?"

"She gave a great deal to me, to everyone."

"Yes, she was of those who gave. She looked about her and gave fully. My feeling is deep and deeply given. I am of a different range."

"I think both things might be said of Mother," said Constance.

"Then we will say them of her. We will say them all. We cannot say too many. I have envied her in my widowhood. And now I am to see her husband widowed. Life is a strange thing."

"It is death that makes it so," said Malcolm. "Without it life would be well enough."

"But it would not be life," said Constance.

"I found it was, before anyone died."

"But death in the background gave it its meaning."

"It prevented its having the meaning it might have had. And so we shut our eyes to it."

"Well, we will not argue to-day."

"So it took Mother's death to prevent Constance and Malcolm from arguing," said Audrey.

"What did she say?" said Eliza, as if she had not fully heard.

"You see I have no feeling," said Audrey.

"She is not herself," said Constance.

"Yes, I am. These things bring out people's selves."

"Yes, indeed they do," said Eliza, with her eyes on her niece. "Indeed I find it so. I feel only love and longing to help welling up within me. I find those are the real things in myself. I can say it with truth."

"I cannot," said Audrey. "I find only different ones, worse than I knew were in me, worse than I knew were in anyone."

"I have never thought of any worse than those," said Malcolm.

"I see that I have them. But it does not matter. It makes no difference."

"Is it not a strange way to talk?" said Eliza, gently. "Try to talk more like yourself."

"I am talking like myself, the self I find is in me. And not like the lowest part of it."

"Try to talk like your mother's daughter and my dear niece."

"What difference does it make to her?"

"We cannot know that."

"I know," said Audrey.

"My child, I cannot bear to hear you. You who cared so much for your mother!"

"That is what it is," said Malcolm. "Cannot you really see it?"

"My dear, I see what you see. How should I not? But we should try to help her."

"It is a good thing it is like this. If it were not, she would suffer more."

"It is the shock that has caused it," said Ursula.

"She will not suffer less for saying what she may regret," said her aunt.

"She will not remember it later."

"But other people may. And that might not be a good thing for her."

"No one here will think of it, in the sense you mean."

"Well, I will not do so either. But I am troubled none the less. I think of what your mother would feel. I cannot quite give up thinking. I am not a person who can do that."

"Aunt Ellen would hardly be happy about any of them," said Malcolm.

"Nor about you, my boy. It is a sad, sad day. I am thankful Miss Gibbon is with them."

"She has lost as much as anyone."

"Well, hardly that. But I know her loss is great."

"The greatest in a sense," said Malcolm, in a lower tone. "They have each other and the future. She has nothing."

"Father will be our object in life," said Constance. "We must forget ourselves in our thought for him. It is what Mother would wish."

"Mother taught us to remember ourselves," said Ursula.

"She taught us many things."

"Not to forget ourselves. She did not want us to learn it."

"I remember her as well as anyone can."

"And do you think I do not?"

"I think you are mistaken about some of her ideas."

"I can only say the same of you."

"Ursula is right," said Malcolm.

"You mean that you think so," said Constance.

"No, I mean what I say. That is what you mean."

"A difference cannot be settled by a few arbitrary words."

"A difference is never settled," said Ursula. "How could it be? It must be there or not."

"Well, I am willing to agree to differ," said Constance, in a moment.

"We cannot be that," said Malcolm. "We have failed to force our view on someone else. And that never finds us willing."

"Well, they agree in so much about their mother," said Eliza. "We will not mind a difference in their memories. There are my boys coming up the drive. They must have come to take me home. They can hardly hope to be of help. How glad they would be, if they could!"

"Verena is with them," said Constance, her tone openly suggesting more than she said.

"And she cannot hope to be of help either. They have come on an unrewarding errand. And they would so welcome a reward."

"Perhaps she has come to see Malcolm."

"Oh, not to-day surely."

"Perhaps especially to-day," said her son. "And whether she has come for that or not, she can stay for it."

"Well, not for long. Your cousins cannot bear with us much further. I had to come to tell them of my sympathy and sorrow. And I take both home with me, and leave one behind. But they need to be alone with each other."

"Verena need not go with you. I will bring her home."

"And leave your cousins?" said Eliza, in a tone of surprise.

"Yes, for half-an-hour. That will do them no harm."

"My boy, you will be a brother to them?"

"A brother may be absent for a space."

"On a day like this?"

"Yes, on any day."

"Malcolm is being a great help to us," said Ursula.

"My dear, it is kind to say so. But you have not known of your trouble long."

"Not long?" said Audrey, on a note of question.

"Malcolm, here is a need that you can fulfil."

"No one can do so. Ursula can do the most."

"Does Verena feel she can do anything?" said Eliza, gently to the latter.

"I help Malcolm by being with him. And that makes him able to help the others."

"Well, that is a great intention. And so my poor boys say nothing. Their feeling has gone beyond words. But their silence carries its message. It will be understood."

"It is a line that suits us," murmured Rudolf.

"My mother's feeling has not done the same," said Malcolm. Eliza looked into his face.

"No, that is outside the sphere where words or silence count. Your cousins and I are in a separate world. I was speaking of your brothers, facing what awed and silenced them. I thought you would understand."

"It has been good of you to come, Aunt Eliza," said Constance.

"And now it will be good of me to go. I have never heard a dismissal put more kindly. And I had already given it to myself. Come, my sons. And, my other son, think of what I have said, and give them of your best."

"I felt you could not bear it any longer," said Malcolm, when he rejoined them. "And my mother seemed to feel the same."

"I did not hear much," said Audrey.

"I think we should recognise the good intention behind it all," said Constance.

"I have been recognising things all the time," said Ursula.

"And recognition is a strain," said Verena, almost with a smile.

"We shall always wish you had known our mother," said Constance, turning to her.

"And I shall wish it. I must try to know her through you. I wish you had known mine."

"Do you miss her very much?" said Audrey.

"I miss my life with her, and am still strange in the new one."

"Do you not enjoy your freedom at all?" said Ursula.

"I might, if I had it. But I do not enjoy the things that go with it, the homelessness and the feeling that I matter to no one."

"You can have that feeling no longer."

"No, I have lost it. I can be myself. I have ceased to be a leaf tossed on the wind. I can look at the future."

"That is what we shall all have to do," said Constance. "It is something to be done for our father."

"Will he not want you to look at the past with him at first?" said Verena, as if speaking from experience.

"Yes, at first," said Ursula. "And it is what we should do anyhow. At first, as you say. But always in a measure."

"I find myself imagining Mother's meeting Verena," said Constance. "It is a useless line of thought. We must live in the real world."

"Most things will never happen or happen again," said Audrey. "That is what it is."

"It is a demand on our courage. But we must rise to it."

"We have no choice. It is necessity, not courage."

"Well, there is no virtue like necessity."

"But necessity is not a virtue."

"I think we can make it one, if we meet it in the right spirit."

"That kind of talk has no meaning."

"It has its own meaning, like any other."

"It is happily only like itself."

"I do not know how to deal with you, Audrey. I am trying to keep my patience."

"And do you feel you are succeeding?"

"Well, it is something added to what we are already suffering."

"If you speak of it with that, you are not suffering much."

"People always say that about other people in trouble."

71

"That does not mean it may not be true."

"It means it is probably not always true," said Ursula. "But we need not compete for the greatest share of grief. We can hardly wish it more than it is. If anyone has a greater, we will not envy it."

"I suppose no two people feel a loss in the same way," said Constance.

"Of course not," said Malcolm. "Everyone's relation with a dead person is different."

"We need not speak or think of Mother as dead."

"We may have to think of her in that way."

"No one need, who does not shut his eyes to the truth."

"Oh, what is Truth?" said Malcolm. "You make me say it."

"We can surely feel what it is in this case."

"You see things too much in relation to your own belief."

"Well, you think you know what the truth is, yourself."

"I face what it seems to me it probably is."

"So do most of us in these days," said Ursula.

"Truth is not altered by the passage of time," said Constance.

"But error may be exposed in the course of it."

"This is not the sort of thing to suggest to Audrey."

"Audrey has thought of such things for herself."

"If I am alone, I am alone," said Constance.

"There is truth," said Malcolm.

"Anyone would think you wanted Mother to be dead."

"No, no one would," said Ursula.

"Mother and I would stand together."

"Constance, you know that is not true."

"We should, now that she knows all there is to be known."

"But that is not what you meant."

"I see that the second is the better way of putting it."

"People always enlist the dead on their side in a difference," said Malcolm. "How often have I heard it done! And they cannot often enlist the living."

"It is borne in upon me that Mother is living and would

be with me," said Constance. "And I do not like this note of dispute on this day of all days."

"There is nothing I like about the day," said Audrey.

"Audrey, that is the tone that troubles me. And I feel that Mother would not be in sympathy with it."

"I think she would," said Ursula. "I remember times when she was."

Constance turned and quietly left the room.

"She is right that we are not observing the day," said Ursula. "But she is happy to be able to do so, to feel that anything matters. So I am hinting something against her the moment her back is turned."

"Well, it is the first moment that is advisable," said Malcolm.

"And Constance does not wait for it," said Audrey. "She uses no choice in moments."

"The young gentlemen!" said Everard.

"We are ashamed of appearing again," said Rudolf. "We have been sent to fetch Verena, and are more ashamed. And we are rendering obedience, and are most ashamed of that."

"So you must behave like the slaves you are," said Malcolm.

"Well, that sounds hard to avoid."

"We behave like heroes," said Nigel. "And it is a heroism that is not recognised in this world."

"And is it in any other? Or is it its own reward?"

"We hardly find it is that," said Rudolf.

"Well, you need show no more. Go back and say I will bring her in my own time."

"Show no more! We could not show so much. Our heroism is not on that scale."

Constance had returned at the sound of guests, and now stood with her eyes on them.

"Verena had better go," she said.

"Why should you deal with the matter?" said Malcolm.

Constance did not turn to him.

73

"Did Aunt Eliza get home safely?" she said.

"They are keeping the truth from us," said Malcolm. "She succumbed to the dangers of the road."

"You will have travelled between the two houses four times," said Constance, with a smile.

"And six times, if we return without Verena," said Nigel.

"Verena, you will save them from that?"

"If they will go on, I will follow with her," said Malcolm. "I would rather walk with her alone."

"Mother said we were to walk together," said Nigel. "Her foresight did not fail."

"She does not want my name coupled with Malcolm's," said Verena.

"You will soon be coupled with me yourself. So we need not consider that."

"Malcolm, had you not better yield?" said Constance. "That sometimes shows the truest strength."

"No, my mother can show it. She has shown enough of the other kind."

"You and Verena walk on, and we will follow," said Rudolf. "We do not mind sheltering behind a woman, when we see no other shelter."

"I could go on, of course. But I am thinking of her."

"Well, think of us, as we are doing," said Nigel.

"I do not mind going first with Malcolm," said Verena.

"Verena," said Constance, gravely, "you are sure you are not doing it to flout his mother?"

"No, I am not at all sure," said Verena, taking Malcolm's arm.

"Ought you not to follow them?" said Constance to the others.

"It is not our scene," said Nigel. "It is fair that Malcolm should bear the brunt of it alone."

"I can understand his not wishing to expose Verena to it."

"Or to expose anyone. We will follow slowly, in case he inclines to be caught up."

Constance looked after them.

"We should not encourage them to talk as they do. We must remember Aunt Eliza is their mother."

"They do not need reminding," said Ursula. "If you think, they never forget."

"I am sure they would not have it otherwise."

"They would have something so, it seems," said Audrey.

"Tea is ready, Miss Ursula," said Everard, who had brought it in unnoticed.

"Tea?" said Audrey.

"You share our trouble, Everard," said Constance. "You will all feel it with us."

"Yes, miss. In our measure."

"It will be a changed home for us all."

"There will be the difference, miss. It had not escaped us."

"Yes, tea," said Ursula, half-smiling. "Something that fulfils our carnal needs. And to-day of all days!"

"Will things go on in the same way?" said Audrey.

"Yes, people will eat and drink as usual. And, what is worse, we shall do the same. And, worse still, they will know that we do. And, worst of all, they will soon say we are quite ourselves again. Well, we can say they are quite *them*selves."

"So Aunt Eliza left without tea," said Constance, as if she would not give ear to these words. "And the time had come for it. It is later than usual."

"Yes, Everard has paid us a certain tribute," said Ursula.

"Well, she can feel we are paying it to her," said Audrey. "We are kinder to her than people will be to us."

"Where is Miss Gibbon?" said Constance.

"She has been gone for some time," said Audrey. "She wanted to be alone. She is too unhappy to be with other people."

"We find it a help to be with each other."

"I suppose we did not give any help to her. Or else she is past helping."

"She can hardly feel more than we do."

"Well, she has nothing left, as Malcolm said."

"I will take some tea up to her," said Constance.

"We can send it," said Ursula. "If she wanted to be with us, she would be here."

"I think she would like to feel we were attending to her ourselves," said Constance, going to the table.

Ursula said nothing, and her sister left the room with a tray, and presently returned with a restrained expression.

"How was she?" said Ursula.

"She did not say."

"Did she accept the tea?"

"She had had some already."

"Had Everard taken it to her?"

"I think she had asked for it," said Constance, looking at the window.

"What did you do with the tray?" said Audrey.

"I left it to be brought down with the other."

"So she will face double discredit. She is as lost to ordinary feelings as that."

"Audrey, this way of talking is not natural to you."

"I do not feel natural. If you do, and it seems you do, you are fortunate. Though I don't know that the rest of us are."

"Well, we will hope you will soon return to your real self."

"This is my real self. What is not natural is to show it."

"I should have thought most of us showed ourselves."

"We show the selves we are accustomed to show, and other people to expect."

"I think I show my real self."

"You show the one you have come to think is yours."

Constance paused.

"Of course there are things we have to conquer in ourselves."

"Yes, you try to improve it and make it better worth showing."

"Audrey, it does not do to yield to bitterness like this. We can feel sorrow without that."

"Few of us, sorrow beyond a point."

"Ursula, can you do anything for this poor child?"

"Only tell her that I feel as she does."

76

"That does do something," said Audrey. "All that can be done."

"I am sure we all feel equally," said Constance. "Different characters must respond in different ways."

"Our characters are certainly different," said Audrey. "Mine is the worst."

"Oh, you cannot be sure of that," said Constance, kindly.

"And Ursula's is the best."

"We cannot be sure of that either."

"I am sure."

"You mean you have formed your own opinion."

"I mean what I say."

"Well, we will not go on. Here is Malcolm coming back, I am sure he is trying to be a brother to us."

"He feels as we do," said Ursula.

"He can hardly feel as much."

"No, but his feeling is of the same kind."

"Well, how did you prosper?" said Constance, kindly.

"That is not the word I should use."

"Did you incur reproof for being late?"

"For being late to-day. It seems that bereavement should involve punctuality. And that was not all I incurred."

"Will it recoil on Verena?" said Ursula.

"No, my mother can be trusted there. She understands where to stop. That is why she can go so far."

"I always say there is something fine running through Aunt Eliza," said Constance.

"I am glad I do not hear you," said Malcolm.

"Why, what is the harm in that?"

"I cannot see it for you."

"Ought I to say that the whole of her is fine? We could hardly say that of anyone else."

"Where is Miss Gibbon?" said Malcolm.

"In her room. She wanted to be alone."

"Did she say so? I somehow cannot hear her."

"I do not know if she put it into words."

"I can tell you. She did not."

"Well, it is not my fault that she has gone. Would you like to go and be with her? This concern for her is a new thing in you."

"The circumstances are new."

"No one would dispute that. I don't know what we are arguing about."

"About Miss Gibbon," said Ursula. "But you need not go on. I hear her door."

"I seem to be the one who should be most often alone," said Constance. "Even to-day you might be happier without me."

"Not happy enough for the difference to count," said Audrey.

"So there would be a difference?"

"You suggested it yourself. I said it was not enough to count."

"That is not quite what you said. I do not know what harm I do you."

"I do not either. But you and I seem to do each other a little harm."

"It may come from our different ways of taking our trouble."

"And from seeing each other's way of taking it."

"Sorrow is supposed to draw people closer," said Constance.

"Perhaps it does not do it on the first day."

Ursula gave a little laugh, and Constance glanced at her.

"Do what on the first day?" said Miss Gibbon, entering and using an ordinary tone.

"Something that Constance said," said Ursula.

"And what did she say? Well, we cannot pick up a conversation in the middle."

"You have been a long time alone," said Constance. "We have been thinking and talking about you."

"We are all thinking about each other."

"I am thinking about myself," said Audrey.

"Well, to-day that is the same thing."

"I should have thought it was a very different thing," said Constance.

"We can take either view," said Miss Gibbon.

"Mrs. Mowbray!" said Everard at the door.

"Aunt Eliza again!" said Ursula.

"Mrs. Malcolm Mowbray, Everard," said Constance, in an incidental tone.

"My expression was correct, miss."

"Oh! Well, it does not matter."

"Say what you have always said, Everard," said Ursula.

"Yes, again, my dear, though it is not quite the word to be expected. I felt I must know how you were after the sad hours. They have been long and sad enough to me to make me wonder. And you had had no tea when I left you, though the time was past. I hope you can tell me you have had it now?"

"I am afraid we let you leave us without it," said Ursula.

"Afraid, my dear? You know how it was. But tell me you have had it yourselves. That is what I want to hear."

"Yes, Everard was later than usual. We had forgotten about it," said Constance. "Did you come alone, Aunt Eliza?"

"No, my boys came with me, but they stayed outside. They would not present themselves a third time. They would hardly have let me come alone."

"That is what I thought," said Constance.

"And you were right, my dear. You had the past to judge by, though to-day the present is enough. Audrey, my poor, pale child, the day is nearly over. You will sleep and forget. You need not promise me to try. Youth and the sorrow itself will help you. At your age there is no doubt."

"I feel there is at mine," said Constance, half-smiling, "though it is not so very different."

"You are wrong, and I am glad to know it. It is Miss Gibbon and I who will keep the night watches. We are not the nearest to the lost one. But in our way we shall be so."

"Aunt Eliza, may we ask the boys to come in?" said Ursula. "I hardly like to think of them outside."

"Yes, if you word the message firmly. Otherwise they may not obey. They have fulfilled their purpose in coming."

Rudolf and Nigel entered, controlling their expressions.

"So you will make the six journeys after all," said their brother.

"Malcolm, that is the first word you have uttered since I entered," said Eliza.

"I thought we had had enough words."

"It would have been natural to speak to me, when I came in."

"It would be more natural, if we never spoke again."

"We must understand each other. No one can come before your mother in your life."

"Someone else comes before everyone."

Eliza looked at him, as though allowing light to come to her.

"Well, my son, then it is to be. It is the second loss in my life. But my life itself is over. The future is not mine. It is yours for you to sacrifice everything to it. Take it for yourself."

"I wish I could make a speech like that," said Rudolf.

"Do you?" said Eliza, her eyes at once alight. "It was made on the spur of the moment. So you are not equal to your mother."

"I was wishing I could emulate her."

"Come closer to her, my boy. You and I will go on together. We will watch other lives and claim no part in them. We shall have enough."

"Have I a place in your scheme of things?" said Nigel.

"My two dear boys! How much we shall be to each other! My three dear boys; for Malcolm must not be less, that he brings me a daughter. I am not less his mother. And it is I who provide her for him. He takes her from me, as he has taken everything. He will come to think of it."

"I had thought of it. And thought you would say it," said Malcolm. "It has no real truth. And is it a time for our affairs to be supplanting those of the house?"

"They are not to me. My mind is on them, though I was drawn aside to glance at yours. My heart is so much with my nieces, that I am going to desert them. It is best for them, and I will not consider what it is to me. I will not even take leave of them. It would be doing something for myself."

Eliza walked home with her sons in silence, and left them at the door of the house. When Miss Manders came to join them, Verena followed her.

"Well, Mandy, there is further change," said Nigel. "We have lost our aunt and gained a sister. Mother has sanctioned Malcom's marriage, and has referred to Verena as a daughter."

"So she has had to accept it," said Miss Manders, with a faint note of pity. "I suppose she could do nothing else."

"She has been forced to," said Verena. "But no one will force me to anything."

"Are you going to repudiate my mother?" said Nigel. "It would be a new thing in her life. I feel a guilty excitement at the thought."

"Beware of being too guilty," said Rudolf.

"I was not used to it myself," said Verena. "And it is a thing that can be remembered. When Malcolm is head of the other house, she may like me to forget it."

"What a line your thoughts are taking!" said Nigel. "Suppose my mother knew!"

"I wonder she does not expect it. Anyone would in her place. She has done harm to her own future. Mine is safe."

"What a way to talk!" said Miss Manders, her mouth unsteady and her eyes going to the boys.

"So you anticipate my uncle's death," said Rudolf. "And he is not an old man."

"It is your mother who has brought me to it. I like elderly men. They have more interest than young ones. And I seem to have it for them. And if it is so with your uncle, I may be nearer to the head of things than she is. She had better think of it. Perhaps she is doing so."

"I am sure she is not. She is engaged with her own life. And she has not a great opinion of my uncle."

"She has of his position. I have heard her talk of it. She seems to resent his having it."

"Well, she would rather her own husband had been the elder son," said Nigel. "She thinks he was the worthier. That is not unnatural."

"And I believe it is not untrue," said his brother.

"I shall find a friend in your uncle. And I shall make a change for him. I am different from his daughters."

"Well, but they are different from each other."

"Not as different as that. They have lived in the same atmosphere. I shall bring in another."

"I think Uncle has enough daughters," said Nigel.

"I am not one of them," said Verena.

"He thinks of Malcolm as a son. He will see you in that way."

"No, I do not think he will."

"Well, brothers and sister!" said Eliza's voice. "So you are getting to know each other."

"We have been doing that for some time," said Verena.

"But not as members of a family. And that is how it is to be. I must not be wise any longer. Perhaps I have been too wise."

"I have not thought you were wise."

"Oh, Miss Manders, this is where you are. I wondered where I could find you. Have you anything to do down here?"

"Well, I had to hear the news. I always come down for that."

"Yes, we expect Mandy to take an interest in us," said Nigel.

"It is sad news to-day," said Eliza. "Their aunt will not return to them. I have been with my poor nieces. Have they told you of the great trouble?"

"Yes, and other things as well. They did not often see their aunt."

"What a strange speech to hear at this moment! That does not alter the loss for her family."

"No, but it puts it further from the boys. They were thinking of things that come nearer."

"Well, perhaps you will do the same," said Eliza, in another tone. "There are things near to you that might claim your attention."

Miss Manders turned to the stairs. Verena took her arm and went with her. Eliza gave them a glance and moved away. And the brothers were alone.

"Rudolf, we have borne ourselves humbly under growing stress. We have rightly behaved as if we did not matter. I begin to apprehend that we do not."

"If they also serve who only stand and wait, we have served indeed. But I doubt if such service is of use. Even the recommendation hardly suggests it."

"We accept a lowly part. But Verena will not do so. She will stand and wait no longer. And she looks at Mother as if she saw her. Can it be that she does?"

"Well, Mother said she would be a daughter to her."

CHAPTER VI

"My dear ones, my now even dearer ones," said Miles, as he embraced his daughters, "my poor, motherless girls! This is an empty meeting for you. Your father returns to you alone. But remember what you will do for him, what you have already done. You have made this homecoming possible. He could not have faced the journey, but for the thought of you waiting at its end, ready to share his grief, to seek his help in your own. And you shall have it, my daughters. We shall tread the empty road together. But for you I must have turned aside, without heart or hope. But we will move forward, striving for her sake, who gave us to each other. Where is Malcolm? Does he not know I am here?"

"He is in the house, Father," said Constance. "I think he meant to leave us to ourselves."

"Yes, that would be his thought. That is what is holding him from me. But let him come. He is as a son to me. He has been your brother in the last dark days. I felt he was with you, when I could not be, when the sad message had gone before me. Yes, fetch him, my Audrey. He is waiting for the word."

Malcolm came from the back of the hall.

"How are you, Uncle?" he said.

"I am well, my boy," said Miles, grasping his hand with especial force, as if in response to something that must be between them. "I am well in body. I am not of those who seek to exalt themselves by claiming they are ill with grief. It is at heart that I am sick."

"My mother would have been here, Uncle. But she thought you would wish to be alone. She will come herself later. Verena is in the house, and is hardly a stranger to you. I have written to you of her. You have written to each other. Even

at this moment I should like you to meet her. You may as
well come to something that is good."

"Bring her to me, my boy. She is to be my fourth daughter.
Who am I to refuse what is offered? I have not so much. I
cannot have too many to help me in my shadowed life. For
its light is indeed gone out."

"I will fetch her, Uncle. I am glad you will see her. You
will be in each other's lives."

"It is true. It is good of you to let it be so. I am grateful to
feel it can be. So, my dear, we meet at a sad moment. You
do not see me as I am. But it helps me to see you, at a time
when I need the help. And you are a sight to gladden an old
man's eyes. May you come to gladden his heart."

"Father," said Constance, as Miles released Verena, with
his eyes still on her, "will you tell us what there is to tell, while
we are prepared to hear? It will be hard perhaps to work
ourselves up again. And it is a thing that must be done, before
we can look at the future. It seems to block the way. It stands
as an obstacle in our path."

"I will tell you, my dear. But what is there to tell? It must
sound a tale of myself. When I came back to life in the house
where I had lain since the shipwreck and all that followed, I
found I had not come back to it. Some had been saved, but
your mother was not among them. My life was over. That is
all."

"We know it is not," said Ursula. "And we know we shall
know no more. It is what we have to be content with. And
we are not content."

"Well, we must be resigned," said Constance.

"How can we be?" said Audrey.

"Perhaps the truth is kept from us in mercy."

"Is that a reason for being resigned?" said Malcolm. "And
it would have been more merciful to avert the tragedy."

"We cannot understand these things."

"We cannot, if we are to see reason in them. It is better
to accept blind forces as blind."

"The troubles may be sent to try us and lead us upwards."

"It is hard on Aunt Ellen to be sacrificed to our advance."

"She might not feel it to be so."

"She would," said Audrey. "And there is no sign of the result."

"My Verena," said Miles, not saying a name that was expected from his lips, "I see tears in your eyes as in those of my own girls. It binds you to us. It makes you their mother's daughter. It makes you mine. God bless you, my four girls."

Miss Gibbon came into the room and looked uncertainly at Miles.

"Miss Gibbon!" he said, just smiling and holding out his hand. "You are ever our good friend. You have been so in these last days. You will be so in those to come. We can ask no more of you."

"How I wish you could, Mr. Mowbray!"

"No more than that is needed. It is much."

"Father, you must eat and rest," said Constance. "Life has to go on. We cannot avoid its customs. They are binding on us."

"It still seems that it all ought to stop," said Audrey.

"I thought so," said her father. "When I returned to life I thought so. I said to myself, 'Why should it all go on? What does it mean any longer? What purpose does it serve?' And it all went on. And I had to go on with it. And I shall have to go on."

"The reason is that we are one family in a world of them," said Malcolm.

"It is no answer for me. It may be for you. You have a purpose and a future, your relation with other lives. I must stand by and see them fulfilled. My life must move on in yours."

"All our lives will move on, Uncle. And not in other people's; in themselves. Whatever happens or fails to happen, if nothing happens, they will move on."

"I will watch them," said Miles. "I will ask nothing for myself. Why should I ask anything? I have had enough. But I would not be a burden. I will do as I am bid. My daughters

86

are in their mother's place. They have bidden me, and I will obey."

"So would most of us, if we were told to eat when we needed to," said Malcolm. "Suppose no one had bidden him!"

"We surely need not talk like that to-day," said Constance.

"I am talking in my usual way, as Uncle talks in his."

"I think he has spoken memorably on the occasion."

"That is what I meant," said Malcolm. "So does he."

"Well, Everard!" said Miles, as he entered the dining-room. "This is but an empty homecoming. I wish I did not bring you only myself. You know how I wish it."

"Yes, sir, it is a change after so long. We have made the observation."

"I know you will do what you can for me and mine. You have had a great loss yourself. You could not have had a better mistress."

"No, sir, as I am called to a position that entails one."

"Will you have someone to sit with you, Father?" said Constance, coming to the door.

"Yes, I will have one of my girls, the one who can best bear with me. I know I am too much for my Audrey. Nay, I am too much for you all. Stay, I will have my fourth daughter, if she will come to me. She will be less affected by my solitude. For her the task will be light."

"I am sure she will come to you, Father. She could hardly hesitate."

"Do not press her, if she does. I have no claim. But I feel that she will come. I have seen her face. We have looked into each other's eyes and exchanged our message. I will await her coming."

Verena came alone into the room, and after a moment sat down by him.

"So my fourth daughter consents to be with me. I will try not to oppress or sadden her. Let her tell me of herself, and I will forget myself in listening. How has she liked her time with us all, her life with Malcolm's family?"

"The first has been better than the second. His brothers have been good to me. But his mother did not want me for his wife. She did not want anyone, or anyone as poor as I am. I don't think she objects to me in myself."

"And I do not think so either. That is hardly a thing that could be. And Malcolm must marry someone, and he is not entitled to so much. He can supply a good deal himself. What is in her mind?"

"Nothing in that part of her," said Verena, smiling. "She does not reason about it. She just follows her instinct. And I believe she thought you would agree with her."

"Well, I do not. The truth is that I seldom do. You will have to learn it soon or late. For the time it is between you and me. It is the first thing we have between us."

"She has given up trying to separate us. Malcolm will not bear it any longer."

"I expect he will not. And neither would I in his place. Indeed I will not in my own. If you want support or help from the source of things, you have it here. You can refer to me, appeal to me, count on me in any way you need. You are as a daughter to me. Come and give me a kiss and seal our pact."

There was the sound of an opening door.

"Why, my dear Miles!" said Eliza. "We could not rest without coming to give you our welcome. You may not feel the need of it. But we felt the need to give it. We admit the need was ours. We were told you would only see your family, but we did not place ourselves outside it. We felt you would accept a wider view. And we see we were right."

"This is one of my family, Eliza. Here is my fourth daughter. Here was a touch of comfort for me on my hard homecoming. Here is another bond between you and me. You are not surprised to find her ministering to me? It was a lighter task to her than to the rest. She had not seen me as I was. And so she can more easily see me as I am."

"Well, I was surprised. But it may be as you say. I am glad she could do something. And she is glad herself, I know.

But as you do not need to be alone, or alone with your family, should we not all be together? You seem to be eating nothing more. It is a little perplexing to me."

"I have eaten what I can," said Miles, rising with a sigh, and laying his hand on Verena's shoulder, in open continuation of his scene with her. "So let us go to your Malcolm and my poor girls. Then I shall have what is left to me. So much and yet so little. I will try to sound less ungrateful. Such a blank and yet so much."

"Is the one much better than the other?" said Malcolm.

"No, my boy, not much better. Nothing can be that. I seem to you to have lost one from many. And I have lost my all. There is no easy way for me."

"Will you not say a word to your nephews?" said Eliza. "They have come, hoping to hear one. And they saw you had them for the newcomer. Though new brooms may work well, we need not discard the old and tried ones."

"I have said no word to them, Eliza. They have said none to me. And we have spoken to each other."

"I am glad that you feel it. We must hope they can do the same. And I am glad Malcolm has been able to serve you. His finding that Verena can help you is a help to us all. We are grateful to him."

"I am grateful," said Miles. "I hope you know it, Eliza. It is a breath of life for me in a world that seemed to be dead, something that tells of light and hope. There is danger in looking back. That will be my peril. I need to be helped to look forward. And in the march of younger lives I feel that my wife moves with me."

"And she does, Father," said Constance. "We shall all go on together."

"I wonder how she likes her manner of progress," said Malcolm. "The rest of us have managed to avoid it."

"That is not as true as it sounds," said Constance.

"How soon do you think of marrying, my boy?" said Miles. "When are you bringing Verena to her home?"

"I hope it may be soon, Uncle. And I thought I might

take her to a home of her own. We both hoped you would help us."

"Well, well, I hardly know about that. That is not quite my view of things. I think we should all share everything that is ours. You share your hopes and your happiness with us. We share our home and what it offers with you. Your cousins will do their part. We move into the future as a family."

"We cannot share the first experience of married life. That must be between ourselves."

"It could surely go on beneath the life on the surface," said Constance.

"I think Malcolm is right, Father," said Ursula. "There is danger in having one household within another."

"And I think he is wrong," said Miles, in a lighter tone. "I do not see the danger. Constance put the matter well. We shall not intrude on each other. There is no mistress of the house to make trouble for a young wife. I mean, your mother leaves an empty place, not one filled by another. And Verena will be mistress here one day. She will be wise to learn her part."

"You are not an old man, Father. It might all go on for a long time."

"And so it might. And so it may. But I find I cannot say, 'May it'. I noticed you did not. I may not be old myself, but my life is old. And the young lives opening about me should send their roots down in their own soil."

"Ursula will be the mistress here in your lifetime, Miles," said Eliza.

"I am not talking about a mistress! The mistress is dead! And all that side of things is dead to me. It died to me with her. I should have thought you would know that."

"It cannot quite be dead to other people. You would suffer yourself, if it was."

"You have many young lives about you, Father," said Ursula. "You do not need another."

"But I do, my daughter. And so do you. It is of all of you I am thinking. You want the leaven of fresh experience in the old, dead life. It had gone on long enough. Your mother had begun to think so. And now it is indeed dead to us."

"Mother always wanted us to have more experience," said Audrey. "But she felt you were against it, Father."

"Well, now I am in favour of it," said Miles, gravely. "If I have ever failed to follow her, I will follow her the more now."

"People who are dead, can give great support to the living," said Malcolm.

"That is a thing you have said many times," said Constance.

"Not as many times as I have thought it."

"Do you expect us to dispute it?" said Eliza. "It is the thing that we have left. We cling to what we can of them. We cannot quite give them up."

"Mother would have been in favour of the separate house," said Ursula. "She used to say that, if Malcolm married, that would be best."

"Used to say," said Miles, almost smiling. "Ah, she will not say anything to us again. We cannot have her advice, my Ursula, my daughter and hers. But she 'used to say' to me something very different. She used to say that life in the house was the best preparation for life at the head of it. Is not that her authentic note? Can you not hear her say it?"

"I heard her say something different. And Verena would choose to have a house of her own."

Malcolm looked at Verena, who said nothing.

"Well, I cannot think any more about houses now," said Miles, with sudden weariness. "I have this house and its questions on my mind. I will go and rest. I should have gone before. I have no one now to warn me that I am not a young man. And I have borne much, more than I should have thought any man could bear. And I have borne it alone. I will not thrust it now on others. They too have borne enough."

He moved to the door. Verena took a step towards him. Eliza hastened after him and laid a hand on his arm.

"Ah, Miles, I know it too well. I have felt that very thing.

You need the companion you have lost, to help you in the loss of her. You need her sympathy in your sorrow. If anyone has suffered it, I have. We will do what we can for each other."

They left the room, and the young people stood in silence.

"I think we have done our best," said Constance.

"We have," said Ursula. "This is our best and the result of it. There is no hope of anything better."

"We can only be what we are," said Audrey. "And things are bad for us as well."

"They are indeed," said Malcolm. "I remember how they were for ourselves. I remember as much as my mother does. They are not things we forget."

"There was the guilt of feeling that our trouble was less than hers," said Rudolf. "That is a thing that the most bereaved person does not suffer."

"But the only thing," said Verena. "And he has to feel he is alone in what he does suffer."

Malcolm looked into her face.

"I need not have wondered how you and Uncle would fare together. It was a simple mistake."

"I think it was a natural one," said Constance. "It is good of Verena to try to understand him. We can see he appreciates it."

"And appreciation is so rare a quality, that we are not at ease before it."

"I wonder if Mother can see us now," said Constance.

"She would not be proud of us," said Malcolm. "We are managing better without her than she would have expected."

"Are we?" said Audrey.

"You are not. It would not matter if she saw you."

"In what way are we doing so?" said Constance.

"We are taking an interest in things that are apart from her."

"I think she would feel she was involved in them," said Ursula. "And anyhow it would not trouble her."

"Perhaps she can see into our minds," said Constance. "Then she would understand."

"We will hope she cannot," said Rudolf. "That is not a thing to be done. Anyhow by anyone who understands."

"Why should we mind, if we have nothing to be ashamed of?"

"Well, then there would be no reason."

"You talk as if you had something to hide."

"As if I had many things to hide, as we all should talk."

"I do not think I have more than is inevitable."

"I daresay I have not either."

"He is sure he has not," said Nigel. "He has been trained in self-esteem."

"I think I have," said Ursula.

"I am sure I have," said Audrey.

"I only hope I hide them," said Rudolf.

"I trust I am not a transparent person," said Nigel.

"I can say that I should not mind, if Mother looked into my heart at this moment," said Constance.

"Think again," said Malcolm. "And imagine her really doing so."

There was a pause.

"Well, perhaps I am not quite prepared for it," said Constance, more lightly.

"You really meant you thought she could not," said Malcolm. "People always betray that they do not believe what they are supposed to."

"Of course we cannot know everything for certain."

"No, there is your line of escape."

"I do not wish for one."

"But you know you have it."

"I think you do not understand what I mean."

"Yes, I do. And you do not mean it."

"I have spoken the truth, as far as it is in me."

"Yes, that is what you have done."

"I think we had better leave the subject."

"Well, we have come to its end."

"And not too soon," said Ursula. "Aunt Eliza and Father are coming."

"Yes, here is your father," said their aunt. "I have brought him back to you. I have done what I can. And he has promised to let it help him."

"Yes," said Miles, with a sigh. "She has done her best. And I hope I am grateful. Little can be done, and so I am the more grateful. It is the thankless task that is the hard one."

"Perhaps I am too exhausted by my own troubles to have much to give," said Eliza, coldly. "I could do no more than my best."

"And you did it, Eliza, and I am thankful. I acknowledge my debt to you. And I am about to ask you to make it greater. Are you going to leave the new daughter with us, to ease our first evening alone? For alone is what all and each of us will feel. Not only Malcolm would be grateful to you."

"Would you rather have her than one of your own nephews?"

"Yea, I would, Eliza. I will speak the truth. It is because she is not my own. She is not related to me. For her the task is light. For her I am not the sad, old man, dragging out his empty days. For her I may have a future as well as a past. She did not know my wife. That gives her the power to serve me, strange though it may sound. She takes me as I am, apart from my grief and what it gathers. And that is more than daughter or nephew can do for me."

"Well, she will stay, of course. Malcolm will be glad for her to help you."

"Why should I be glad?" said Malcolm to Ursula. "Why should Uncle ask so much of her? Why should I wish her to give it? People only have a certain amount to give."

"That seems to be the truth, as regards ourselves."

"I think we did not quite realise what Father needed," said Constance.

"Neither did he, until he met it," said Malcolm.

94

"Ah, my boy!" said Miles, looking at his nephew as though guessing his words. "You are reluctant to grant me the one thing of yours that can be of help. Well, I will not ask it. I have no claim. It is not mine to take, but yours to give."

"I should like to stay with your uncle, Malcolm," said Verena.

"You mean you would like to stay with us all. That is what it is."

"Yes, with you and all of them. It is what I meant."

"I think there was an especial message to me," said Miles. "I think I heard it."

"You probably did. It was put in plain words," said Malcolm.

"Well, goodbye, Miles," said Eliza. "We will leave you now. And I am glad we leave something with you to ease your way. Malcolm will bring Verena back to us."

"No," said Miles, just shaking his head and speaking almost musically. "I will bring her. It is I who have asked for her, asked something of her. It is for me to do so."

"I shall take her, of course," said Malcolm.

"Of course," said his uncle, smiling and speaking at once. "But it is a sign of what she has done for me, that I can speak even in feeble jest. Feeble it was. I shall not jest in my old way again."

"Have you ever jested?" said Malcolm. "I should not have thought it was your habit."

"With your aunt, when we were alone. You did not hear it. There were things we shared together."

"Surely not that," said his nephew.

"No, I must say I cannot imagine it, Father," said Constance.

"It is I who do so," said Miles, in a dreamy tone, looking at the window. "It is all I can do now. Imagine things as they were."

"Father," said Constance, "if we do not always do what you want for you, we may feel you will tell us? We should only be glad to hear."

95

"That is a rash assurance," said Malcolm. "It is a thing that seldom gladdens."

"But you do, my dear ones. Different people do different things. You do your own dear part. Even your aunt does that. And I do not know why I should say 'even'. I am thankful to many. I were an ingrate, if I were not."

"I am already not gladdened," said Ursula.

"I hope we do justice to Aunt Eliza," said Constance. "I think in her own way she does it to us."

"Why will people do things in their own way?" said Audrey. "The ordinary way is best."

"I have thought she did not do it to me," said Miles. "But I see her with a new eye. She has tried to rise to my need. If sorrow makes us sensitive to kindness, it also seems to bring kindness about. She may be thinking of me at this moment. I feel I am in her mind. And I am not often wrong in such things."

Miles was not wrong now.

"What a strange mood your uncle is in!" said Eliza. "It is natural that he should not be himself. But the change takes such an odd form."

"It seems to liberate something in him, that has been suppressed," said Rudolf. "It is as if a barrier is broken down."

"It almost is, though I hardly like to say it. I do not know what to make of him."

"I wonder if I do," said Rudolf, in a low tone to his brother. "I hardly like to say it either. Indeed I will not."

"Neither will I," said Nigel.

"Well, how are things in the other house?" said Miss Manders, when she joined them.

"As would be expected," said Nigel. "Except one thing. Verena has found favour in Uncle's sight, and is staying to support him."

"Well, she is a stranger, someone from outside," said Miss Manders, in a tone of sympathy. "That is what he must need."

96

"He has just come from outside, himself."

"But he has come to everything he has always had. He must be thankful for someone who is apart from his trouble, and sees him apart from it. He cannot have nothing else."

"How you understand everything! That is almost what he said himself."

CHAPTER VII

"THIS IS SOMETHING that perhaps I ought not to say," said Constance. "But I feel I cannot keep it to myself."

"Of course you cannot," said Malcolm, "when that is the reason. And we fear there may be others."

"Well, you will not misunderstand me. But is not Father seeing a great deal of Verena?"

"We will not do so," said Audrey.

"Of course I do not mean to imply anything."

"Then we did misunderstand you," said Ursula.

"You mean that he feels her attraction," said Audrey. "And is yielding to it."

"I did not intend to be as definite as that."

"No, to define a thing seems to give it substance," said Ursula.

"I do not mean that anything could come of it."

"No, of course not. Who would dare to mean it?"

"Malcolm, cannot you do anything about it?" said Constance, in open appeal.

"I have done what I can. And if anything more could be done, I will not do it."

"No doubt it will fade away. I do not see what else could happen."

"None of us can," said Ursula. "To see a thing we have to face it."

"Perhaps we should be glad that Father is meeting with help in his trouble."

"We ought and were. But it is no longer true. The trouble has become the opposite of itself."

"You do not mean it has in a way become an advantage?"

"We must begin to mean something. It has left the road clear."

"We should surely put such thoughts out of our minds. We are not the better for them."

"I agree that they are not exalting."

"And we ought not to grudge anyone his happiness, least of all our own father."

"We can grudge him selfishness and folly and the indulgence of them."

"It may be that thoughts of ourselves are creeping in."

"That is hardly the word. They are open and undisguised. And there is nothing wrong about them."

"Perhaps we ought to put ourselves quite aside."

"It would be letting other people do the opposite. That is what Mother would have said."

"It somehow seems sacrilege to speak her name in the connection."

"It is certainly not one that invites it," said Malcolm.

"Yes, even the distance things have gone, seems to involve insult to her."

"What involves insult to whom?" said Miles, striding through the room. "Why are you all in solemn conclave?"

"We were thinking about our life without Mother, Father," said Constance.

"Oh, that is it! Well, it will have to be without her. There is no help for it. Things must take their course."

There was a pause.

"Perhaps that was not quite straightforward, Father. We were not exactly talking in that way."

"Well, do not be straightforward. I know what that always means; something besides the straightforwardness. And I have no fancy for it. But what was it about something's being an insult to someone?"

"Well, perhaps not a conscious insult. We were thinking that something seemed in a way to involve one."

"Very few things involve anything else. Any real thing must exist of itself. Words that lead to such confusion are used too much."

"They soften the truth," said Malcolm. "And it sometimes calls for it."

"How many shall we be at luncheon?" said Ursula. "Do you know if Verena will be here, Father?"

"No, I do not," said Miles, with a touch of triumph. "But one person does not make much difference."

"If only that were true!" murmured Audrey.

"Perhaps Malcolm knows," said Constance.

"No, he does not," said Miles, controlling a sharpness in his tone. "He has been in the library this morning. He cannot have seen her."

"That is true," said his nephew. "I do not know."

"She is sure to be here," said Audrey.

"Then why was there the question?" said her father. "And why is she sure to? She was not here yesterday."

"That is what Audrey meant, Father," said Constance, quietly. "She does not miss more than one day."

"Then Ursula knew what to expect, and could arrange accordingly. Your words have no meaning."

Constance went on in the same tone, looking at no one.

"Would it not be as well for Verena to change her seat at the table? And sit by Malcolm instead of by Father? She is too intimate now for conventions to count. And that is her natural place."

"A guest sits by her host," said Miles. "It is better not to break the rule. A breach of convention tends to be a breach of manners. There is reason behind all custom. And we should never presume an intimacy. It is a road to danger."

"She is coming up the drive," said Audrey. "This is her usual time."

Miles turned at once, and with a reckless air of disregarding the opinion of his family, strode into the hall. Malcolm had turned at the same time, but recalled himself and was still.

"Father is getting more open in his—tactics," said Constance. "I suppose we ought not to want him to be surreptitious. But his impulses seem to betray him. I wonder how long it will go on."

"Why should it stop?" said Audrey.

"It must either go further or wear out," said Malcolm, and followed his uncle.

"Poor Malcolm, I can imagine him," said Constance. "I know what he is doing. Passing Father and Verena as if he did not see them, and then just giving them a glance! One's heart goes out to him."

"I wish we could give them a glance ourselves," said Audrey. "Do you think we might?"

"Audrey! Even in jest that is going too far."

"It was going further. It was not in jest. But Father has set us on the downward path. How do you suppose they met?"

"Oh, one's thoughts shy away from it," said Constance, shuddering and turning aside.

"A glance is the only thing," said Ursula, and moved to the door.

"Ursula! You of all people!"

Ursula opened the door and suddenly withdrew from it.

"What is it?" said Constance. "One ought not to ask. But everything seems to be in chaos."

"Oh, nothing. They are only coming arm-in-arm along the hall."

"And is that the first thing they did?" said Audrey.

"They look as if it may not have been."

"What is the joke?" said Miles, as he passed with Verena. "I was glad to hear the mirth. I had had my glimpse of gloom."

"A joke never bears repeating, Father," said Constance.

"No, I daresay not. But I am glad you are in a mood for one. There is nothing against your being so. A conscious clinging to sadness is a poor thing, unworthy of the person who causes it. And it is a poor course to serve the past. We should look to the future, meet it full and fair. It is the braver thing."

"It may call for courage," said Ursula.

"Then show it. We may want it in different ways. And I hope we shall not fail. To meet sorrow needs it. To admit a return to happiness needs more. To face someone else's happiness needs the most. And I have thought of you as having it."

"Malcolm cannot rise to that pitch," said Constance, as the steps went on. "Of him it is asking too much."

"Verena was quite silent," said Audrey.

"And Father was not," said Ursula. "And silence does not really say more than words."

"Surely he will turn back in time," said Constance. "In justice to Mother, to Malcolm, to Verena, to all of us. And in justice to himself most of all."

"People do justice to themselves in different ways. And I fear they always do it."

Malcolm returned to the room.

"Malcolm, we think Verena should sit by you at the table," said Constance, speaking to fill the silence. "The circumstances call for it."

"It depends on what you feel them to be."

"Would not Verena herself prefer it?"

"She could say so in that case."

"She might be afraid of repulsing Father," said Audrey.

"That would be the result of doing so, and the point of it."

"Malcolm, cannot you do something?" said Constance, once more.

"I do what I can by being here. My presence is all I have to give. It is at once not nothing and not enough."

"Well, all in confabulation?" said Miss Gibbon, entering and speaking easily.

"What else should we be?" said Ursula. "Either with each other or ourselves?"

"Miss Gibbon, what can we say or do?" said Constance. "Is there any help for us?"

Miss Gibbon spoke in urgent tones.

"Only what you can give to yourselves. I see no other kind for you. Could you not go to your father, and remind him that that is what he is? And beg him to remember it in time?"

"Could we?" said Constance, standing up straight, with her hands rigid and still.

"We could," said Ursula, "if we could face the likely failure, and meeting Father after we had failed."

"Well, it can be nothing worse. And we can meet it together."

"And our present situation is hardly a success," said Audrey.

"Are you coming with us, Malcolm?" said Constance, moving to the door.

"No, not at once. But I am glad you will go, and grateful to you for going. And you can do no more than fail."

"I suppose Verena is still with Father," said Audrey, as they crossed the hall.

"We cannot help that," said Constance. "We must strike while the iron is hot. I mean, while our courage is keyed up to the needful pitch. If we wait, it will falter."

"Mine has done so," said Audrey, falling back.

"Father," said Constance, moving forward, and glancing at her sisters to hold them to her support, "we have come to ask something of you."

"No doubt you have. You would hardly come to offer me anything. It would be the first time."

"Father," said Constance, continuing as if she had not heard, "we beg you to pause and consider before you go any further. You know what I mean. You will not pretend you do not."

"It will pretend nothing," said Miles, glancing at Verena and causing himself to smile. "It is you who are in that danger. You pretend to be honest and high-minded. And you are really cold-hearted and concerned for yourselves. Why should you beg anything of me? Would you expect me to do the same to you? Would you even now, when I might feel the need? And why should I think of you so much? Who thinks of me but myself and one other? I must take what is given. I cannot live with nothing. And I have not anything else."

"I have not either," said Malcolm, from behind his cousins. "And only one of us can have it. One of us must live with nothing."

"Father, you have your daughters, your home, your memories. Surely they are not nothing."

"Memories are less than nothing. They mark the lack in the present. And what have my daughters been? What have they given me but sorrow and pain and emptiness? They thought they were the right things for me. And I was to have them for my life. Is it any wonder that I turned to something else?"

"Father, it was all we had ourselves. We thought we should share it together. We would have given you sympathy, affection, companionship. But you turned from us to another."

"And she does not give me sympathy. She prevents my having need of it. Which must I like the better? I do not want you to tell me. What use would you be to me? Malcolm can take you back to your own place."

"Well, was it any good?" said Miss Gibbon.

"We can hardly say what it was," said Ursula. "Good is not the word."

"You feel it was a simple failure?"

"It was not simple," said Audrey. "It was different things. And Verena did not say a word. It was hard to know what she thought. Perhaps our hope lies there. Could we appeal to her by herself? That is, could Constance do it?"

"Well, I advise you to leave nothing undone."

"That is a demanding course," said Ursula. "And she is always with Father."

"He goes to the farm before luncheon. And she waits for him in the library. He will be going almost at once."

"So there is no excuse for postponing it. And it asks nothing of me. But what can be the end for Constance?"

"We must face it," said the latter. "We must not let our courage ebb. And it is the lesser of the two trials."

"You have great courage," said Miss Gibbon. "How I wish I could be of help to you. But I must see you do everything alone."

"We are Mother's daughters," said Constance. "We can only remember her and remember it."

"That is a great word," said Malcolm.

"It must be on all our lips."

"But it was not," said Ursula. "It was on yours."

"It is being Father's daughters that is our trouble," said Audrey. "And it seems unfit, when he has ceased to regard us as such."

"I think we need not go as far as that," said Constance. "Let us turn our minds to our second ordeal. We are acting in Father's interest as well as our own."

"People are said to be blind to their own interests," said Malcolm. "I have always wondered how the idea arose. But I hope this is a case of it. Anyhow you are acting in mine. And this time I cannot support you."

Constance led the way to the library, where Verena was alone. She was sitting at the desk, arranging its contents, a thing hitherto done only by Miles himself. She looked up as they entered, and did not speak, giving them no help with their purpose.

"Verena," said Constance, "you know what we would say. The thing we have said to my father. Cannot you resolve to face and follow the straight path? And so be more truly bound to each other than in any other way?"

"Did you say that to him?" said Verena.

"Not those words. But he knew our meaning."

"So you see we must be bound to each other?" said Verena, controlling a smile.

"We see what we must," said Ursula. "And we know only what we see. We hardly know how much you know yourself."

"I know the moment. And I am going to live in it. A life is made up of moments. I meet them as they come."

"But the moments are made up of other things," said Audrey.

"Yes, and some of those are needless and useless and harmful to suffer and remember. Your father and I can have no more of them. This is the last."

She returned to her task, and the sisters could only leave her.

"Well, was it any use?" said Miss Gibbon.

"We hardly know," said Constance. "I think it may have been."

"Why do you think that?" said Ursula.

"Well, I feel that our best, honestly done, must achieve something, that a hard effort, honestly made, cannot wholly fail."

"Have you any other ground for hope?" said Malcolm.

"There is none," said Ursula. "The hard effort failed. And I knew it would be hard, when I left it again to Constance."

"We cannot be certain," said the latter.

"And uncertainty is said to be the worst thing of all," said Audrey. "And we cling to it as the best. Or we should, if we could see any."

"What we fear is surely impossible," said Constance. "It is unfitting and humiliating, and even absurd. I think those are really the words."

"They are," said Ursula. "But impossible may not be. It is seldom the word."

"Well, the trials are over. We can feel we have done our utmost. And no one can do more."

"People seem inspirited by that," said Malcolm, "even when nothing has resulted. It all seems to be a waste."

"Ursula," said Audrey, in a low tone, "has Constance enjoyed doing her part?"

"I hope so. It had to be done. And you and I would not do it, because we should not have enjoyed it."

"Was she really acting a scene?"

"She was seeing and hearing herself. So she must have had her reward. I hope Father will not forget it."

"I shall not," said Audrey.

CHAPTER VIII

"Now i know there is going to be a scene," said Miles. "I do not expect anything else. If you like, I have no right to. If you like, I have brought it on myself. That is to say, the opposite has happened, and forces outside myself have carried me away. We really have no control of them. We are borne onward, as I have been. I know I have. I do not deny it. I do not deny anything. I admit it all; my age, my widower-hood, my family, everything that can be said against me, though why it is against me I do not know, nor how I can help any of it. And I admit there are forty odd years between Verena and me, though if you will tell me how to help that, I will hear you. And I admit we are going to be married. That is, I tell you of it, and am proud to be able to. Now it is out, and you must make what you can of it. And no doubt you have foreseen it, though you have pretended to be half-blind. So now let the storm break. I know there is going to be a storm."

Miles was wrong. There was silence.

"We could not believe the evidence of our eyes, Father," said Constance, at last.

"Well, now you can believe that of your ears. I have done all I can for you. I have said what I have to say. And I am ready for you to do the same. Get out what is seething within you. I think nothing of this ominous hush. I am not in the least baffled by it. So that is what you were planning, the battery of silence? Silence was to be stronger than words. Well, you will find it is not. As it says nothing, so it does nothing. I am not impressed."

"Anything that can be said, goes without saying," said Ursula.

"Oh, it does, does it? Then let it do so. I am sure I am

glad to hear it. I have no wish to have it all hurled at me, to stand as the target for all your criticism and ill-will. I see no advantage in it. But let it be words or silence. I can accept either. It makes no difference."

"Your daughters have done nothing wrong, Miles," said Eliza. "There is no reason in the tone you take. And of course it is hard to accept the truth."

"And I have done nothing wrong either. So do not take the line that you don't accept it. Because you do, or you would not all be standing there, transfixed like pillars of salt. And why should I not do as I choose with my own life? Whose is it but mine? Anyone would think it belonged to all of you, to see you all aghast at my living it. I have lived it too much for other people. And I am faced with the result. What are you going to do with your own lives? Live them for me or not? Answer that question, and the matter is at an end."

"We have always done our best for you, Father," said Constance. "Especially since you have been alone."

"Yes, we know what you have done. Lived in my house and taken what it gave. Alone is what I have been. You would have left it, if you had wanted to or had the choice. And I should not have prevented it. And you will not prevent what I am doing for myself. So you can realise it."

"Have you thought what it will mean to them, Miles?" said Eliza. "To have Verena in their mother's place?"

"In their mother's place! She will not be in it. She will be in her own place. A new place, a new life, a new chapter; that is what it is to be. And they can look forward to it. Why should they not do that? I have seen many signs that they have had enough of looking back. And I am in sympathy with it. We do nothing by serving a memory. We can do everything for the living and nothing for the dead. Ellen used to say that."

"What would Ellen say to what you are doing now?"

"Oh I thought it would come to that. That is the meanest thing that could be said. And so of course you say it. People can be trusted for that. And anyhow you can, Eliza. I would depend on you in some ways, if not in all."

"Verena is not here," said Constance, looking round and saying no more.

"Of course she is not. Would you be here in her place?"

"If I could be in such a place, I think I should like to take my stand in it."

"You claim too much. You are not a stranger to me."

"I begin to think you are to me, Father."

"Of course I am. We none of us know each other. And you need not take me to task for contradicting myself. Because I don't need the information. And it has no truth."

"Do you understand the life it will be for Verena?"

"Yes, I do. And it will be the life I choose for her. Not the one you have it in your mind to make it. A life in her own house, and at its head, supported by me, protected by me, filled by me with all that can be given. What else should it be? What else would you expect? And if anyone tries to prevent it, I shall devise means to make her repent. And in my place that would be easy. So I hope you understand."

"It is no good to ask what you have said to Malcolm, Father," said Ursula.

"No, it is not. Because I have said nothing to him. And I shall say nothing. Why is it for me to say anything about a woman's changing her mind? Surely she may do that. I thought it was recognised among men that that was accepted, and no comment made on it, or anyhow no criticism."

"You can hardly expect a man to say nothing, when his promised wife is taken from him."

"Then I do expect it. That is just what I do expect. It is not the part of a man to say anything, to obtrude himself and his wishes for his own life. He is supposed to stand aside and forget himself. That is what I should do in the place, and I expect another man to do the same."

"Would you have done that, Father," said Constance, "if Mother had been taken from you?"

"Have you listened to what I have said? Then you do not need an answer."

"I am saying nothing," said another voice. "You need not fear."

"And I did not fear, my boy," said Miles, turning and using another tone. "I did not fear for a moment. I knew you would behave like a man, and let a woman lead her own life without harassing or troubling her. When I took you into my house as my heir, I knew as much about you as that."

"Malcolm may not remain your heir, Father," said Constance.

There was a pause.

"Have you anything else to tell us, that no one knows but yourself?"

"I think it was natural to say that."

"There is something it is better to say. He will remain many things to me."

"Should we just ask if Verena would like to say anything?" said Eliza.

"No, you should not," said Miles. "And you know it as well as I do. You mean that she would have to say something, that you would wrest something from her. Oh, I know what you mean. You would not let her off without forcing some effort from her, some discomfiture on her. I know how you women are to each other."

"You have not found that in your own family, Father," said Constance.

"Then do not let me find it now ."

"Yes, I have something to say," said Verena, opening the door. "I have heard what you have said. Who had as much right to hear it? Who is as much concerned in the matter as I am? It is the rest of you who are pushing in where you have no place. I am going to marry Miles. I find he is more than anyone else to me. I always hoped I should marry a much older man. I shall always be grateful to Malcolm. I will try to do my part by you all. That is all that need be said."

"And it is well said, my dear," said Miles, taking her arm and guiding her to the door. "And the only thing you will have to say. I will see it is. I will shield you from risk of this kind. I will ensure that you are left in peace."

"May we ask how soon you think of being married, Miles?" said Eliza.

"No, you may not," said Miles, looking back. "Why should you ask all these things? I do not ask any of you. I daresay you would like to ask me how soon I think I may be buried. Ah, and now I know what you will all say. That I should ask myself that question. I can see it in your eyes. Well, I shall not ask it. I am going to look forward and take my part in the future, as you are yourselves. And all who live in this house, will reconcile themselves to it or seem to. And that is my last word."

"I almost feel it ought to be," said Rudolf. "This is my first."

"Do you remember that we foresaw this, Mother?" said Nigel.

"I remember you hinted something about it."

"We were half in earnest," said Rudolf. "And we shall never have the credit."

"You deserve none. You did not really expect it. And it could not have been asked of anyone."

"Did you honestly foresee it, Rudolf?" said Constance.

"Well, not honestly. But I really might have been more surprised."

"I could not have been," said Audrey, "even though I knew it. Even now I cannot believe it is true."

"My Audrey, that is your first word," said Eliza. "And Miss Gibbon has also been silent."

"I can only think of the years behind us, Mrs. Mowbray."

"We shall always have those to look back on," said Constance. "No one can take them from us. And I do not mean to imply that Father would wish to."

"Verena called Father 'Miles'," said Audrey.

"My poor child!" said Eliza.

"No doubt you will all get used to it," said Malcolm.

"My dear boy!" said his mother.

"You did not want me to marry Verena. The ill wind is doing its work."

"My dear, dear boy, you know how your mother feels with you."

"I suppose we have no choice but to accept it," said Constance.

"Do not keep any alternative to yourself," said Malcolm.

"We must feel that Father has a right to order his own life."

"No, that is too simple," said Ursula. "It might condone too much."

"I almost found myself saying that I wished Mother was here."

"That would indeed mend matters."

"We can never think of Verena as Father's wife," said Audrey.

"You will do so more, when the children come," said Malcolm.

Eliza gave him a look almost of fear.

"If a boy is born, I suppose I shall return to you, Mother."

"Well, your home always waits for you, my son."

"It is very hard on you, Malcolm," said Constance. "That must be said."

"Why must it? It is the last thing that would naturally be."

"My poor boy!" said Eliza, putting her hand on his arm. "Come with your mother and be at home and at peace."

"No, he will not go with his mother," said Miles, striding back into the room. "He will stay here in his own home. Cannot you forbear rushing into the future, and foreseeing and discussing things like village sluts? If Malcolm should not remain my heir, I should secure his welfare. He would keep his work here and his place in our life. What do you think I am? One of yourselves?"

"Would it be possible for him here, Father?" said Constance. "With Verena placed as she will be."

"He will get over that. He is not a girl. And you will give up that tone in talking of my future wife. You will accept the position and be friends and sisters—friends and companions to her. Do you understand me?"

"Yes, Father," said Constance, her eyes on the closing door.

"Well, your question is settled, Malcolm," said Ursula.

"It is for the present. Words are only what they are."

"We can hardly be sure of anything," said Eliza. "Another force has come in. I think I should have a talk with Verena herself."

The door again broke open.

"No, you should not," said Miles. "And you will not. I hope you will not dare to. I forbid it. I have a right to. I will protect her from such a purpose. You will not speak of her marriage, unless she does so. You will obey me in the matter. I impose my command upon you. You are one of the women of my family and owe me obedience at its head. And you will not question it."

There was silence while the door closed.

"Mother does not do so," said Rudolf. "It is a strange occasion."

"A happy one for you," said Malcolm. "Make the most of it."

"I hope Verena understands what she is doing," said Eliza. "We are in a way losing hold of her. And she is in my charge."

"Do not risk the door's opening again," said Nigel.

"The lads are excited, Mother," said Malcolm. "It makes a change for them."

Eliza did not meet his eyes.

"Verena may come to wish she had not done it," said Audrey.

"I am troubled about her," said Eliza. "Her mother trusted her to me."

"Then be worthy of the trust," said Miles, in a quieter tone, through a door set just ajar.

"Miles, that is what I want," said Eliza, starting forward. "It is what I am trying, and feel I am failing to be. Does she realise that she is shaping her life, that it is a matter of her future?"

The door closed again, and Miles's step left it.

"Well, it has come to pass," said Ursula.

"And it is no such surprising thing," said Malcolm. "Old men are known to be attracted by very young women."

"Your uncle is hardly old," said Eliza. "And Verena is barely a woman. Her life is at stake. But yours is free, my son. And you will learn to live it."

"I am to do so in the house where Verena is married to Uncle. He is inclined to state his opinion of us. What is ours of him?"

"We must just await the future," said Constance.

"An unusual occupation," said her cousin.

"More so than it sounds," said Ursula. "It does not often lose its meaning like this. And we seem to have no present."

"I must say it once more," said Constance. "What would Mother feel, if she knew? Of course we cannot be sure that she does not know."

"I wonder if Uncle is sure," said Rudolf.

"I am sure," said Ursula. "So there can be some advantage in unbelief. I thought there was none."

"I suppose Father was lonely," said Audrey. "But then so were we all."

"Not as lonely as he was," said Malcolm. "He had no one of his own age."

"And has he now?"

"Well, marriage seems to make its own difference."

"Are we really so surprised?" said Ursula. "Of course, I know we are. But ought we to be? We might have known him better. I don't think he disguises himself. If Verena had not been here, it might not have been so soon. If no one, it might have been never. But the possibility was there."

"It is wisdom after the event," said Nigel.

"Well, events add to our wisdom. And we see we have not been wise."

"We should go, my sons," said Eliza. "We forget that this house is not ours."

"And we have to remember it is Father's," said Constance. "And that he can do as he chooses in it."

"We shall hardly need reminding," said Ursula.

"I mean, of course, as long as he does nothing wrong."

"And you feel he is fulfilling the condition?"

"I should be ashamed to feel it," said Audrey.

"Who will fetch Verena for me?" said her aunt.

"You mean, who will face Uncle for you?" said Rudolf.

"I will go and fetch her," said Malcolm, moving to the door.

"No, surely that is not necessary, Malcolm," said Constance.

"Well, it seems it will be useful."

"It hardly will," said Ursula. "Father will take her home himself."

"He is coming," said Malcolm, moving backwards. "I suppose it need hardly be said."

"I will ask him where she is," said Eliza.

"No, you will listen to him. I guess his purpose. It is to put things on a better footing."

"Well, we should not hinder him in that," said Constance.

"And we can imagine an improvement in the present one," said Audrey.

Miles entered, threw himself into a chair and spoke in an ordinary tone.

"Well, we shall soon have another member of our household. Things will be moving forward."

"We almost have one now, Father," said Constance. "Verena is here a great deal."

"And is there anything against that? If she can be here for one person, she can for another. What is the difference?"

"The forty-four years in your ages," said Audrey, with a sudden effort.

"Now," said Miles, in a deep, almost growling tone, sitting forward with his shoulders hunched and his head seeming to protrude from them, "is this going to cease? Because, if not, I am going to make it. Do you all hear me?"

"Yes, Father," said Constance, in a faint tone.

"Am I in your power, or are you in mine?"

"Do you realise," said Ursula, "what a mean thing that is to say?"

"Yes, I do. And I realise what mean things I have had said. I do not forget a single one of them. It is as if they were burnt on my brain. I see that I need another person in my life. If anything could confirm it, you would do so. A set of poor, little people without perception or pity! Content that a man should drag out empty days, as long as theirs were untouched! And that man their own father! It is a lesson I shall not forget."

"That is not the only way to see the matter," said Constance.

"You did not see it at all. You saw yourselves blocking the path. Well, you can move out of the middle of it. It is your place no longer. What are you crying for, Audrey?"

"It is not for Mother. It is not only for her. There is nothing left."

"We will do our best in the new life, Father," said Constance. "We needed time to accept the idea. It was a strange one to us."

"You will, will you? Well, you can hardly avoid it. There is no one to support you but your father. But I don't want to say mean things. I have heard too many of them. They are an evil part of human life."

"Have you any idea when you will be married, Father?" said Ursula. "It is a thing we shall have to know."

"Yes, as soon as possible. To cut short this trying interlude. It will leave too much behind, if it continues. We shall not be able to get over it. Whether or no you meant to prevent the marriage, you have hastened it."

"I suppose you will have a quiet wedding?" said Constance.

"Not a wedding at all; a simple marriage. We do not want anything else. Verena would not have it."

"That is what I should have expected, Father."

116

"Well, I am glad something is to your mind."

"That will certainly be best, Miles," said Eliza.

"Now what an odd thing the marriage service is!" said Miles, leaning back and using an almost confidential tone. "I have been reading it. And I can hardly believe that I have heard it pronounced over myself. I mean I had forgotten that part of things. It is only a passing ceremony."

"Well, twenty-six years have followed on it," said Ursula.

"Now, now!" said her father, lifting his hand. "That is enough. There is the same thing again. You seem to be so full of it, that it escapes you in spite of yourself."

"It was surely an innocent thing to say, Father," said Constance.

"No, it was not innocent. And you know that as well as I do. I am tired of hearing thrusts in every speech. I am going to have a change from it. I have been thinking of asking Verena to come here until we are married. It will be better for her and all of us."

"To this house, Father?" said Constance.

"If you know of any other, tell me of it. I know of none." There was a pause.

"It is not a usual arrangement, Miles," said Eliza.

"Why, a girl is often a guest in the home of her future husband. What is there against it? Miss Gibbon and my daughters will be here. There is no breach of convention."

"But those visits are usually short ones."

"Well, this one will be longer. That is the only difference."

"Does she think of being married from this house, Father?" said Ursula.

"She can return to your aunt's for that, if it is better."

"What will Malcolm do, Father?" said Constance, in a grave tone.

"What do you mean?" said Miles.

"He can hardly be in the house with you and Verena."

"Why not? He must be in the end. But he can go back to his mother, if he chooses."

"It is a good thing I have a house," said Eliza.

"But I do not see any reason."

"There is none," said Malcolm, with a frown at Constance.

"What does Verena say to the idea?" said Eliza.

"She is relieved by it. She dreaded the time in your house, and did not disguise it. So it is for me to save her from it."

"Well, we have no choice in the matter, Father," said Constance.

"No, you have not," said Miles, in an almost complacent tone. "I am in the superior place. And I tremble to think what my fate would be, if I were not."

"The fate of such people is not of the best," said Ursula.

"Oh, and in what way does yours not please you?"

"You can hardly need to ask that."

"Well, yes, I know," said Miles, with a note of mingled sympathy and satisfaction. "But I am going to do as I choose. Things are taking a new turn for me. I begin another chapter in my life. I may have years before me. There are not so many behind."

"You are sixty-five, Father," said Constance, in a tone that made no comment.

"Well, that is not eighty."

"I expect Nigel thought it was," said Rudolf. "At his stage he sees no difference. And I believe I did not see enough."

"We must go, my sons," said Eliza. "Is Verena coming with us?"

"No, she is staying here," said Miles. "Will you arrange about her things?"

"Let us go at once," said Nigel, as his mother said nothing. "Too much is being kept from Mandy."

"Miss Manders?" said Miles. "I have a word to say about her. Tell her I am grateful for her kindness to Verena. I shall remember it and hope to repay it one day. I don't know what she would have done in that house of yours without it."

"We certainly cannot give that message, Miles," said Eliza.

"Then say something that conveys my gratitude," said Miles, nodding at his nephews. "It can be put in any form."

Nigel put it as his uncle had, as he repeated his speech to

Miss Manders, word for word. The latter listened to it, as she considered Verena's clothes.

"So we lose everything here. The other house is to have it all. There will be nothing left."

"Malcolm will be more with us," said Rudolf. "He will not want always to be there. What do you think of the news?"

"Well, I knew it was coming. Poor Malcolm, it is hard for him. It was not right of your uncle. I don't think we can say it was. What a state of things! Suppose Mrs. Mowbray came back!" Miss Manders smiled, as she envisaged this contingency.

CHAPTER IX

"WELL, HERE IS the future mistress of the house," said Miles, as they came to the dinner table. "She can sit by me for the present. But I shall soon see her opposite to me. She will be apart from the rest of you. She will be one by herself. And I shall be glad not to see that place empty. We feel we have to keep our eyes from it. It seems to stare one in the face."

"It should be Ursula's place for the time," said Malcolm.

"Well, but she has not taken it."

"We left it empty, Father," said Constance. "To us that is what it was. We have kept our own places."

"Well, there will be none to be affected by my marriage. That is something gained."

"Perhaps Aunt Ellen's ghost is in the place," said Malcolm. "Or will be, when Verena comes to it. It is a Shakespearean state of affairs."

"What did you say?" said Miles. "Say it again."

Malcolm repeated his words.

"Do not say such things. Do not hurt and upset someone who is innocent and helpless. It is an unmanly thing, mean and revengeful. It makes me ashamed."

"I was trying to make a joke, Uncle."

"It is a strange thing to joke about. I could not bring myself to it. Though the emptiness of the place has driven me to fill it, and I admit I am finding my reward. I have some sense of what is fitting, of what is due to the past. As I said, you make me ashamed."

"I might say the same to you."

"Malcolm, this is unworthy of you."

"Again I might say the same. It appears that we ourselves are not so worthy."

"I blush for this acrimony and womanish spite. I would not have believed it."

"There is much that I would not have believed."

"Come, that is nonsense. Our lives have to go on."

"Mine has ended," said Malcolm.

"No, no, it is only at a standstill," said Miles, in a different tone. "It will gather force. Think of mine a while ago. What was it for—for how long?—for quite a time?"

"It is true that it has shown a power of recovery."

"The time between your coming home and your actual engagement is just eighteen weeks, Father," said Constance.

"And eighteen weeks too long. If you thought I was going to live in that way, you were mistaken. And if you wanted me to, you were worse. I daresay you were both. Where is Miss Gibbon?"

"She has gone to see a friend," said Ursula. "She has one not far away. She has been to her more than once."

"Well, I am glad she has someone to visit. It will make something in her life. I often feel she has not too much."

"I don't think she would like to be pitied, Father," said Constance.

"Pitied? Who is pitying her? She needs ordinary concern. I have thought she seemed unsettled lately. And I am glad she is to have some change."

"I agree that she does not seem herself, Father. She seems to be disturbed, and to be trying to suppress it. Perhaps the change in the house troubles her. She may be afraid for the future, and feel she must turn to her friends."

"Miss Gibbon has come home, miss," said Everard, "and has gone to her room. She said she was tired and would rather not have anything. But something was taken to her."

"That is right," said Miles. "You will see she has every attention. Now we are a lifeless family. Verena might be with us every day of our lives, to judge from our behaviour."

"She soon will be," said Malcolm. "There is no reason to make an event of her presence."

"You might not have wanted us to be in evidence, Father,"

said Constance. "We wondered if you and she would like to have dinner alone. And then there seemed to be objections, and we did not suggest it."

"Oh, well, that was a thought. But we must get used to being with you all. We shall be alone sometimes. We might be so later in the evening. Well, my dear one, how do you like the prospect of ordering this household? Do you feel it will be too much for you?"

"No, I am not alarmed by it. I think I shall take to management. And you will be behind me."

"Will Verena do the housekeeping?" said Audrey, with an involuntarily note of surprise.

"The cook can do it," said Ursula, lightly. "And Verena can have the credit."

"Who has done it since Aunt Ellen died?" said Malcolm.

"The cook. And I have had the credit."

"I can do it," said Verena. "I shall do all I ought to do. I shall claim no credit that is not mine. I should not take a place, if I did not mean to fill it."

"You cannot have had much experience," said Constance.

"Did she say she had?" said Miles.

"No, Father. And I did not say she did."

"You implied that she suggested it."

"I simply stated that she could not have had it."

"I have not," said Verena. "But I shall not need it. These things are not a matter of experience. They are either in people or not. And I feel they are in me. Many things are, though no one but Miles has seen them."

"I don't think I am good at showing what is in me," said Constance.

"Oh, I don't know," said her father, in his grim manner. "I should have thought you had shown a good deal."

"I was speaking of capacities, Father."

"Your father was not," said Verena, with a light in her eyes.

"I hope we are not to continue in this strain all the evening."

"You have made your contribution," said Miles. "You can cease to make it."

Constance did not do so. She hardly seemed to have the power. And at the earliest moment Ursula rose from the table.

"Well, my beloved, what are we to do?" said Miles. "Shall we follow someone's suggestion and go and be alone? It is what people do in our position. Shall it be the library or the drawing-room? Where are the rest of them to be?"

"So that is our future status," said Audrey.

"In the schoolroom, Father," said Constance. "We feel inclined to be there to-night. It is a room with its roots in the past. I daresay Miss Gibbon will join us. So you can feel happy about her."

"Well, it all fits in. It leaves the drawing-room free. And that will be Verena's place. Tell Miss Gibbon that I hope she will soon be herself again."

"I do not think Father was at ease at dinner," said Constance, as they went upstairs. "I hope we did our best for him."

"Ursula did," said Malcolm. "And I had to see her doing it. And you did your worst. And I had to see that too. It made a degrading sight. He has you in his power."

"I did not mean to make things difficult for him."

"Then I am glad you did it unawares. He should not have them easy."

"It is hard to see the future," said Ursula.

"I should not have thought so. We have had a clear glimpse of it."

"I think Verena has a will of her own," said Constance. "And her own ambitions for the future."

"They would hardly be anyone else's," said Malcolm.

"And a higher opinion of herself than appears at first sight."

"We can most of us disguise it as long as that."

"She is glad to have scope and power," said Ursula. "And it is as well she has something to look forward to. She is not doing a wise thing."

As the sisters reached the landing, the door of their mother's room opened, and Miss Gibbon came out, carrying some clothes.

"Oh, Miss Gibbon! You are clearing Mother's closet!" said Ursula. "I knew it would have to be done. I have kept putting it off. I am glad you have faced it. It is a burden off our minds. I think we need not ask Father about it."

"Ought he not to know?" said Constance.

"He ought, but we will spare him."

"Malcolm would say he should not be spared."

"It is no good to try to be revenged on him."

"Aunt Eliza said she could use some of the things. She saw we should hardly wear them ourselves, or care for them to be worn by strangers. She would like the shawls and cloaks, and will find them useful. If Miss Gibbon will give them to me, I will send them to her in the morning."

"Oh—I cannot give them to you, Constance. I cannot let you have them. I have disposed of those things. I have given them away—to someone who needed them. I ought to have asked you, but the matter was distressing, and I said nothing. I thought it was better to attend to it. And I was just dealing with the other things."

"Oh, that is as well. We are glad it is done," said Ursula. "I hope they will be useful. Aunt Eliza will understand."

"I think she was only trying to help us," said Constance.

Miss Gibbon turned quickly away, and left a silence.

"How unlike Miss Gibbon!" said Audrey. "I should not have believed it."

"It would have been natural to ask us," said Ursula. "But the matter is better behind. I do not understand it. But I see that people are not to be understood. It is wise to give up the idea."

"Is she giving the things to the friend she goes to see?"

"I suppose so. No doubt she is. But there is no need to ask her. It would make an awkward moment, and she meant no harm. So that is what she was doing, when we thought she was resting! What an atmosphere of discomfort and mystery there is over everything! It is a strange day. But life has become strange."

As the schoolroom door closed on his daughters, Miles came up the stairs. It was his purpose to fetch something from his room, and at the same time to enquire for Miss Gibbon. He found the latter's room empty, and entered it to await her. His eye was caught by some clothes on the table, and he approached them, drawn by instinct and memory. A piece of wrapping paper, directed for the post, and a written letter lay near them; and he took up the letter, impelled to know where the familiar things were to be sent. He read it, read it again, turned pale and took some steps about the room. Then he paused, took pencil and paper from his pocket, copied the address and went into the passage. When Miss Gibbon appeared, he made his enquiry and returned to the drawing-room.

"Ah, my Verena, how I need you! How I need your right in the future, your protection from the threat of fate! For it menaces us and lies in wait. We cannot walk straight forward. We are halted and flung back. We make our way in the dark. And then we cannot bear the light. And we should not be asked to turn towards it."

"You are an orator, Miles. There are many things unrecognised in both of us. We must show people what we are. Your family have not known you. And they are less inclined to know me. But they will not have the choice much longer."

"My family are not with me, Verena. And he who is not with me, is against me. It is a hard thing."

"They shall not be. I will not have it. They are old enough to do better than they do. They may not want you to marry, but how could you help doing something of the kind? How could you live in this atmosphere of ill-will and egoism, asking and getting nothing for yourself? If they wanted to keep you, they should have done it in a fairer way."

"I think I may say that such things, if they existed, were the result of the change rather than the cause of it," said Constance's voice. "I came to ask you something, Father.

But perhaps you would rather I did not, as you are not alone."

"Why, you knew I was here," said Verena. "And anything you have to say to your father, can be said before me. We shall not have secrets from each other."

"Then, Father," said Constance, keeping her eyes on Miles, "we wondered, on second thoughts, if we ought to consult you about something. Do you agree to Miss Gibbon's sending Mother's clothes to friends of her own, who need them? We found she was doing so, and gave our consent. And then we felt that the matter did not only concern ourselves. Do you give your sanction?"

"Yes, of course," said Miles. "She may do as she pleases and thinks fit. After all her years with us, it is her right to do so. You need not have asked my consent. And she need not have asked yours."

"Thank you, Father. She does not know I have done so. We just wanted to be sure. Why, Father, how pale you are! Is anything wrong?"

"It is this medley of hostile emotions all round me. I feel I cannot get away from them."

"You cannot, of course," said Verena. "They must be controlled. We must all put a better face on our feelings. Your daughters are not the only people who have them. They think they are, and that there is no reason to hide them. But they must either conquer them or manage it, as I have done. You bear too much."

"Perhaps you have been patient in your way, Father," said Constance, slowly. "But we have all had to meet a demand. We can all try to do better."

"Then do so. You have your opportunity. Come down from that fastness and live up to your words. My hour with Verena is spoiled now. I am all unsettled and distraught. We shall have other times together. Come down from that room, where you are too old to be, and where for years you have not been, as you know very well. It is an act, and not a well-natured one. It can come to an end."

Constance left the room with a set expression, taking her father at his word.

"They think you don't mean what you say," said Verena. "You have said too much without enforcing it. You must teach them better."

"I must indeed. We must return to our old footing. We have somehow lost it in the last months. When once that is done, the first hurdle is passed. Come in, all of you, and accept your promotion to the drawing-room. Come in, Malcolm, if you can behave as if you were grown. Miss Gibbon, I am glad you are equal to it. You have had enough of the schoolroom in your days. Are you still feeling tired by your journey?"

"No, not very, thank you, Mr. Mowbray. I have only been to another village. But it was enough for one day."

"What village was it?" said Constance.

"Now Miss Gibbon will go where she chooses, when she chooses, without being questioned," said Miles. "She is mistress of her own actions. And if she needs any support, she is entitled to mine."

"She has only just begun to have it," said Ursula to Malcolm. "So it is to be a new life for us all."

"You brought up the subject yourself, Father," said Constance.

"Well, now I will change it. And in future it will be avoided. Miss Gibbon can make her own plans."

"Thank you, Mr. Mowbray. My duties are certainly elastic. I only hope I have enough of them."

"You do what needs to be done. And that is to do everything. We ask for no account of it."

"Has Miss Gibbon somehow got Uncle in her power?" said Malcolm.

"We might think so," said Ursula, "if she had any power. And she seems to have gained some."

"Father seems different," said Audrey. "Is he remembering the day when he first brought Mother to the house?"

"No, he is not," said Miles. "Oh, I heard what you said.

No, I am not remembering it. She would not think I should or ought. I remember *her* better than you do. Malcolm, cannot you take that cloud off your face? You might as well cry like Audrey."

"Well, so I might."

"Why cannot you behave like a man?"

"That is what I am doing, as she is behaving like a woman. As you say, there is little difference. We are both human beings."

"And a poor thing it is to be, if this is a sample of it. I have only met two people in my life, who were worthy of the name."

"And by marrying them both you fare well," said Malcolm.

"Well, you wanted to marry one of them. That is a thing I would not say, if you did not goad me to it. You seem to want to force it from me. A woman is allowed to make her choice. I have said it before, and I say it again. And I hope it is for the last time."

"I hope so too," said his nephew.

"I think you are over-tired, Father," said Constance.

"In that case he needs rest," said Verena. "And it is not what he is having."

"Oh, a few words do not make all that difference."

"Oh, don't they?" said Miles. "A few words can make or mar a human life. Whether they are spoken or written, they have the power."

"You must learn not to listen to them," said Verena.

"So I must. You and I must go on together. We must keep our eyes on the path ahead. We must look forward."

"We should look both forward and backward," said Constance.

"I think that is what we do," said Miss Gibbon.

"It is the braver thing to look in front," said Miles.

"So Uncle's doings have needed courage," said Malcolm.

"They must have," said Audrey. "I can't think how he has dared."

"I dreaded the evening," said Constance. "But not for the right reasons. I shall be thankful when it is over."

"I hope a lifetime of such evenings is not before us," said Ursula. "I knew that one must be."

"A new gloom is over things," said Malcolm. "There does not seem any reason for it. And it seems to come from Uncle himself, hardly the person to be causing it."

"Who is that at the door?" said Miles, in a sharp tone.

"Mrs. Malcolm Mowbray and the young gentlemen," said Malcolm.

But it was Eliza by herself.

"Now I know I am not expected. So I have come alone. That is, I have left my attendant sons outside. They naturally would not let me dispense with their protection. I have come to enquire for my charge, and to bring her a message from Miss Manders. She looks happy and at home."

"That is what she is; at home," said Miles. "And she is not alone in being happy."

"I am glad you are so too, Miles," said Eliza, resting her eyes on his face. "And I hope they will all come to be."

There was silence, and Eliza continued.

"So you have had a journey to-day, Miss Gibbon. I heard you came back by the local train. Was it a successful expedition?"

"Yes, thank you, Mrs. Mowbray. I did what I wanted to do."

"I suppose you went to friends? You are fortunate to have some so near. Are they family friends?"

"Well, I have known this one for a good many years."

"Has it been a long parting?"

"Not so very long."

"Has she come lately to the neighbourhood?"

"Well, she came back to it not long ago."

"How do you know it is a woman, Aunt Eliza?" said Constance.

"Well, it seemed more likely. Miss Gibbon might prefer a woman friend. I wish I had one myself."

"Now I have said it before," said Miles, "and I say it again. I will not have Miss Gibbon catechised about her doings. Her time is her own, and she is answerable to no one for it."

"Why, Miles, I was only showing a friendly interest. She might ask the same things of me."

"So she might. And so she shall, if she wishes. But we know she will not. She will leave you to go your own way without comment or question. She knows the world well enough for that."

"Why, Miss Gibbon, we shall scent a mystery. You will have to unravel it for us."

"There is no mystery," said Miles. "And if there were, she would not want to divulge it. And she should not be asked to."

"You will have to tell us who your friend is, Miss Gibbon, and everything about her."

"No, she will not," said Miles. "I knew it would come to that. Questions, questions and no chance of keeping her own counsel! She will not have to tell you anything, and will not do so. And that is enough."

"It is indeed," said Eliza. "There was hardly need of so much."

"Poor Miss Gibbon!" said Constance. "What shall we be thinking about her?"

"Think what you like," said Miles. "And keep it to yourself. No one will ask you."

"I think my nieces are looking pale," said Eliza. "And indeed so is their father. And Verena is flushed. But I must not make enquiries."

"Verena is excited when Father is there," said Audrey, in a low tone. "Why does she feel so much for him? As much as I suppose she does?"

"We must say there is something likeable about him," said Constance.

"That is what Audrey meant," said Ursula. "That is, she did not mean any more. Verena is flattered by his attentions and by the idea of being mistress of the house. She has been in Aunt Eliza's house, where someone else is mistress."

"We must feel it is something more than that. That seems such a trivial thing, apart from the surface."

"It does not to her. It is the promise of importance and power. And she considers the surface of things."

"I don't think there is any harm in her."

"I daresay there is not. But there is ambition to rise and outshine other people. And that may work harm for her."

"Whispering!" said Miles. "Whispering and questioning! The two unforgivable things! And we seem to have nothing else."

"Of course we have whispering," said Malcolm to Ursula. "What is there about any of it fit to be uttered aloud?"

CHAPTER X

"WELL, THE DAY is fixed. Your aunt and I are agreed. Everything is complete. A week from to-day Verena and I will be married. And three weeks later we shall return to our home, to a new life and the old one, the old one and a new. And a happy one for all of us, if you will let it be. It will depend on you. Verena and I will do our part. She will consider you all, as if you were her daughters——"

"No, it cannot be in that way, Father," said Ursula.

"We have wondered when it was to be," said Constance.

"Well, you have not had to wonder long. We have not wasted time. It is not such a while since we first saw each other."

"It is not, as we have said before, Father."

"Well, you need not say it again. It is a thing I can do for myself."

"We shall always remember your return to us, Father, our feelings when we saw you come up the steps alone."

"Well, this time when I come up them, it will not be alone. And if you are not glad of it, you are no daughter of mine. And if you show it to me, I shall cease to see you as one. I warn you in time."

"This has been rather a shock to us. It is not usual for a widower to marry again so soon."

"Nothing is usual about it," said Miles, with a touch of complacence. "It is not usual for a man to marry a woman so much younger than himself, or usual for her to accept him. It is not our object to be usual. We are content to be what we are, to follow our own path. And I don't know how it is, Constance, but whenever I talk to you, there is this feeling of guilt and discomfort. If our marriage does not make an end of it, I must devise some means of doing so. And you can bear it in mind."

Miles left the room, and his daughter's eyes followed him.

"Father seems always to misinterpret my words."

"He interprets them," said Malcolm. "And it is fair that he should have to. But his marriage will make a difference. Things will be irrevocable and permanent, and words will have no power."

"Or only his words will have it," said Ursula.

"I still feel that it cannot happen," said Audrey.

"We are still unsure of our attitude. Everything seems to involve something that is a wrong to someone. And nothing is fair to ourselves."

"If only Mother were here!" said Constance. "I cannot help saying it. I mean somewhere in the background, to help us with her counsel."

"We may as well think what it would be," said Ursula.

Miss Gibbon started forward.

"You can have it, Ursula. You must know the truth. You have a right to know it. I have a right to tell you. I cannot hide it any longer. I should never have hidden it. It cannot be hidden, now that this marriage is upon us. Your mother can come to you. She is not dead. She was saved as your father was, but was ill longer. She was unconscious and was parted from him, and only knew the truth, when she came to herself. She is well and can return to you. She can give you her counsel, give you your lives again. You have wished for her so much and so often. You will have her now."

The silence seemed to be alive.

"Are you sure?" said Ursula. "Tell us the whole truth."

"She wrote to me and told me everything. She asked me to break it to you. She had come to a village not far from here, to be on her way home. She did not know what had happened, and I had to tell her. I went to her and told her myself. And she would not come back to us. She did not know what to do. She was weak and unable to judge like herself. She wondered if she ought to leave your father to his life. I told her it could not be, but she would not hear me. She bound me to silence. She forced me to give her my word. I have broken it now. I could not help it. What could I do, with the future threatening as it is? I ought to have broken it before. I ought never to have given it. I have gone on, not knowing what to do. I cannot go on any longer. She must not go on. Truth is always best."

"It is, when it is a truth like this," said Malcolm.

"Mother will come back!" said Audrey. "It will all come back. Everything had gone, and it will be ours again! Nothing can matter any more."

"Has Mother had money to live on?" said Ursula.

"It is a strange thought to come at once," said Constance. "But I was just going to ask."

"It is not at all strange," said Malcolm. "So was I."

"She had some with her. I could give her a little more. And then someone who must have known about it, sent her money. She has no idea who it is. I have no idea. It is all I can tell you. It is all I know. I am thankful it is told."

"So these days are over," said Ursula. "The world is our own place. To think we shall live in it! In our old world."

"We shall know better what it is to us," said Constance.

"And you took Mother her clothes," said Audrey to Miss Gibbon.

"Yes, I took her some, and sent others. You remember that night."

"So we know all," said Ursula. "And Father knows nothing."

"He can soon know all," said Malcolm.

"I cannot help feeling sorry for him," said Constance.

"We ought to be able to be glad," said Audrey. "Will he be glad for himself?"

"How can we tell?" said Ursula. "We can only assume that he is. There can be no other course. And he should know at once."

"Why should he know anything?" said Verena's voice.

"Why should it not be as Mrs. Mowbray said, if she is really alive and said it? Why cannot he be left to the life he longs for with a young woman, instead of being thrust back into a dead life with an old one? You know what he needs. You cannot have been with him in these last days without knowing. He has shown what it means to him to live with youth instead of age. You are heartless daughters, but you cannot have shut your eyes and ears. You have not done so. I have seen it. You have often betrayed yourselves."

"That is the talk of a child," said Malcolm, moving towards her. "You and my uncle are forced apart. You can only face it and forget what has been between you. It is you who will have youth with you instead of age. You who should have it! Don't you see that the other thing was against truth and nature? You will return to me and to a life that will withstand the years. The other would have fallen before them."

"I am going to marry Miles," said Verena, with steady eyes and her voice deep. "I will not go back and be under everyone again. I am not fitted for a subservient place. The marriage is to be in a week, and when it is over, nothing can be done. Mrs. Mowbray chose to remain concealed, and she can do so for the time that is left to her. After what she has suffered, it cannot be long. There is nothing against it. She has seen it herself as the only moral thing. If she is what you all say, she was bound to see it. People need not speak of what they know. Everyone knows something that is never said."

"No one does," said Audrey. "Things are always said."

"We should indeed be heartless daughters," said Ursula. "You will find your judgement of us is wrong."

"And the marriage would not be valid," said Constance. "It would mean nothing."

"It would be worse than that," said Malcolm. "It would be a breach of law."

"Not if Miles did not know about it. And he need not know. No one need ever know."

"Of course it would become known," said Audrey.

"You mean you would betray it? And you think you are not heartless. What do you think you are?"

"Of course she means that," said Ursula. "And she would be heartless, if she did not. And of course I should betray it myself. And so would Malcolm and Constance and Miss Gibbon. We could not give up our mother. It is a thing that need not be said. Father will see it as we do, or would, if he were like anyone else. He should be thankful to have his wife again. We cannot help it, if he is not."

"He is a person by himself," said Verena, weeping. "You know what he will suffer, and suffer without any sympathy. I could do all that he needs for him. I could give him some happy years before he is old. And you will sacrifice him and me. It is an evil thing."

"How I wish Mother was here!" said Constance. "Now it is a thing that may be said. How soon can it be true?"

Malcolm turned to Miss Gibbon.

"I will do what must be done, what should have been done before. What will give them back their lives and give me back mine. And give you back yours. Yes, and give Verena hers. I will go where you tell me, and I will not come back alone. I must leave my cousins to deal with the problem here. Women can only have the worst part. They must somehow tell their father."

He went to the door with Miss Gibbon. Verena waited for a moment and then rushed out of the room. At first the sisters were silent.

"It is true that it is the worst part," said Constance.

"But everything is coming back," said Audrey. "It had gone, and it will be ours again. All of it with nothing different."

"We must not think of it now. There is this to be done before we can look forward."

"If there was not, it would be too good to be true. Something must save it from being so. I suppose Verena is not with Father?"

"No, she has gone upstairs."

136

"Then let us get it over. If we put it off, it will get beyond us. We shall begin to feel pity for Father, and that will confuse everything. He has not felt any for us."

"It needs courage," said Constance. "And of course we feel pity for him. That is why it needs it. And we must be careful to keep any exultation out of our tone. We do not want to make it harder than we must."

"It is strange that we feel it is a sort of triumph for us. Instead of a happiness especially for him."

"I feel pity for his predicament," said Ursula. "No one has been in such a one before. Not so much for anything else. We have had to give too much to ourselves."

"Won't he be glad at all to have Mother back?" said Audrey.

"The strange thing is that we do not know. And we do not dare to think. It seems that he must feel a certain gladness. He could hardly care for her for all those years to have nothing left. The question is whether it will be lost in other feelings."

"I could not tell him. It cannot be asked of me. I can hide under cowardice and custom, as I have always hidden."

"I could not either. It is the worst thing to have to embarrass him. And this is embarrassment on such a scale. We seem to want a stronger word."

"It does need courage," said Constance again. "But I ought to be able to show it. Someone must do it, and it will keep it off anyone else. That should be enough for me. Is Father in the library?"

"Alone," said Ursula. "Verena has not come down."

"How sorry ought we to be for her?" said Audrey.

"Not so sorry as glad. She will come to be glad for herself. She will see Father become an old man. And if she marries Malcolm, she will be mistress here one day."

"We do not know that she thinks in that way," said Constance.

"I think we know that she will."

Constance approached the library with a pale face and

hesitant step. She was not wrong that it needed courage. Her father's aspect did not help her. He was sitting at his desk, his usual position when unoccupied, and so a familiar one. He was tapping his fingers on it and looking out of the window.

"Father," said Constance, coming up to him and using a gentle tone, "I am going to ask you a question."

Miles turned sharply towards her.

"No, you are not. I am tired of these hints and suggestions under an innocent guise. I will not hear it."

"I think you will, Father. And I think you will answer it. Indeed you will have no choice. It is a simple question. If you could ask one thing for your own life, what would it be?"

"What kind of thing? You know what I ask. And you know I am going to have it. What is there behind it?"

"We shall come to it. Go back further. Go back to the beginning of things, to the foundation of your life. What would you ask?"

"That I should have been younger when I met Verena?" said Miles, with a frown. "I am making no sacrifice of her. She does not feel it. You know she does not, and you know that is the question."

"No, go back to the root of things, Father, to the basis of your experience. What would you ask?"

"Oh, you know I cannot have it. That your mother should come back to me? It is an empty question. It has no meaning. The answer must be as empty. Will you leave me alone to tread my own path? It is the last time I shall say it."

"It is, Father. You will not need to say it again. You will not be able to. The question is not empty. It is a real and vital one. And the answer is what came to you. Tell me what you would ask. Because it is to be given you."

"What?" said Miles, rising to his feet, with his face charged with realisation. "What? What are you saying? What is in your mind? How much of it is there and nowhere else? What is the truth?"

"Father, I will tell you. Indeed I think you guess. It is a

great truth, as great as it can be. Mother is alive and will come back to us. She will soon be with us. We have only to be ready to welcome her."

"Tell me the whole," said Miles, sitting down. "That means very little."

"She was saved as you were, Father, but was ill longer. When she came to herself, she moved to a village on the way home. She wrote to Miss Gibbon and asked her to tell us the truth. Miss Gibbon went to her and broke to her the truth on our side. And Mother would not come home. She was weak and unable to judge. She thought she ought to leave you to your future. She made Miss Gibbon promise to be silent. Miss Gibbon went to visit her. She gave her what money she could. She took her her clothes. You remember she gave them to someone. You remember the night when I told you. And some unknown friend sent her money to live on. Then your marriage was upon us, and the silence had to be broken. Mother must come to us, Father. Malcolm has gone to fetch her, to bring her to her home, to the daughters who wait for her, to her husband, Father. The sad, false chapter is over. We can go back to the time before you left us, and then left us in another sense. Let us return to it together. Let us have our father again as well as our mother."

There was a long silence, and then Miles spoke in a low tone.

"There is someone else to be thought of. You cannot have forgotten."

"Verena knows, Father. She heard Miss Gibbon tell us. She was startled and said things that had no meaning, and then ran away. But we must not think of her. She will have another life. Malcolm will give it to her, a life more fitted to her and her youth. And you will have the life that is yours. Father, turn your eyes to it. Take it back with both hands. Remember how you felt, when it was torn from you. Look back at that time, and you will find you can look forward."

There was another silence, and then Miles rose again, put his arm about Constance and led her across the hall to her sisters. His voice came low and even, almost as if he were quoting what he said.

"My daughters, my three dear ones, who have seen my grief, seen my effort to mend a life, that was broken beyond my power to live it as it was, you will stand by me and with me in the hour to come. For my hour will not be as your hour. It will be fraught with sorrow and question. It will be strange with its own strangeness. I seem to be destined not to live as other men."

"So it was something as dignified as destiny," murmured Audrey. "And it need not be referred to Father at all."

"We shall stand together, Father," said Constance. "We shall welcome Mother as the family we are. Of course we will leave you alone with her at first."

Miles heard the words in silence, and turned and left them. As he went towards the library, Verena came through the hall. They started, stopped, moved forward as their eyes met, and then Verena hurried on and out of the house. They knew that their next meeting would be in another world.

"I hardly think Father was grateful for your promise," said Audrey to her sister.

"We surely need not use that tone to-day."

"We are too keyed up to be natural," said Ursula. "We must get through the hours as we can."

"We are not to see Father and Mother meet," said Audrey. "We have only what is good before us. There is nothing to dread."

"I feel no hope for the meeting. Father himself feels none. He has mastered many moments. But they will not help him with this."

"The first hour will soon be over," said Constance. "And our real life will begin. I did not mean to spare ourselves, when I said we would leave them alone, but to spare Father. And so perhaps to spare Mother even more."

"What a pity there has to be the sparing!" said Audrey. "It might have been so different. But nothing can matter now."

The hours of the day went by. The sisters remained together. Miles stayed apart from those who were not afraid, feeling too apart from them to seek their presence. He feared for the minutes to pass, followed the hands of the clock, prayed in the actual words that the cup might pass from him, heard his speech to his daughters as hollow and without hope.

CHAPTER XI

THE MOMENT CAME and passed before they knew. Malcolm led his aunt into her home. Miles hastened out and held her to him, remaining in the hall for the protection of its gloom. Both were grateful that no one saw or heard.

"My husband, you are still that to me?"

"My wife, I should always have been so in my heart. I found the emptiness too much."

"I did wrong not to come to you at once."

"You did wrong, my Ellen. And you led me to another wrong. We will never do wrong to each other again."

Ellen almost felt herself smile, as she led him rather than let him lead her, across the hall, and met her daughters with the feeling that was natural. There was the normal constraint and silence, and Malcolm broke it with any words that came.

"Would you like to be left to yourselves, Uncle?"

"No, my boy, it is your right to be here, and our right to have you. And we should have Miss Gibbon too. Her place is with us. We will not be grudging with our happiness. It is not only ours."

"It is ours first of all," said Audrey. "And it will always be."

"Ellen, this daughter has done ill without you. And none of them has fared well. They could not even try to fill the void, as I did, and did in vain. They could do nothing."

"It perhaps gives us more now," said Constance.

"We all have all we can have," said her father, gravely. "We will not apportion the shares. Come, Miss Gibbon, you are one of us. Here is our family complete."

There was silence, as someone else entered their thought.

"To think we only knew this morning!" said Audrey. "The other time seems to be fading away. If only that could happen!"

142

"It showed us what we had," said Miles. "It had its use. It proved to us the vanity of trying to mend a broken heart, a broken life. A broken thing must be left to lie in its fragments."

" 'Sweet are the uses of adversity'," quoted Constance.

"We did not find them so," said Ursula.

"They may have led us upwards."

"They did the opposite," said Audrey. "We are better already for the difference."

"We are happier. We must try to become better."

"I shall not try. I feel I have suffered and deserve amends. And it is coming true."

"Yes," said Miles, "it is a full and fit reward. Sorrow, mistakes and mistaken effort are all wiped away."

"So Uncle accepts his deserts," said Malcolm to Ursula. "But I wish he would not talk about them."

"It is the best thing he could do. I was afraid of the worst, afraid of silence. I should have thought the demand would be beyond anyone. It would have been beyond anyone else. How much he has that is his own!"

"I wish he had more that is possessed by other people."

"You are silent, my wife," said Miles. "But your silence speaks. We do not need your words. We know what is in your heart, as we feel the echo in our own."

"With Uncle something else speaks," said Malcolm. "Not silence."

"Mrs. Malcolm Mowbray and the young gentlemen!"

"Well, Everard, you share our gladness," said Miles. "You have your mistress again."

"Yes, sir, it is averted. It will be like former times. We have remarked upon it."

"I look forward to seeing you all," said Ellen. "Will you tell the others?"

"Yes, ma'am; we are all here. It happens that change has not ensued."

"My dear sister, what a sudden joy! And what a joy to welcome you! It was a thing I could not leave undone. Though word was not sent, it came on the wings of love. How thankful they must be! How thankful I am for them and with them for this healing of their hearts and their lives! My son, I have a word to say to you. Verena is to be my daughter. She has come back to me in a twofold sense. And she will stay with me until you claim her."

"Eliza, we thank you and welcome you," said Miles. "You shared our sorrow and you share our joy. You saw our struggle to mend our life, and you see it made whole again."

"Is there nothing Uncle cannot carry off?" said Nigel. "I imagined his position as impossible."

"And looked forward to seeing it so," said Rudolf. "I am relieved to be spared. But how did he face Aunt Ellen? I don't mean it taxed his powers, but I shall have to know."

"He did not face her," said Malcolm. "He met her in the darkness of the hall. It may be fortunate that the hall is a place of greeting."

"What are you whispering about?" said Eliza. "You should be thinking of your aunt and her return."

"Our uncle also gives food for thought," said Nigel. "What were his feelings when he heard he must expect her?"

"You must remember that he had thought she was dead."

"That was certainly involved in his purposes."

"Oh, I know what it is, Eliza," said Miles, with a sigh. "I know what they are saying. How should I not know? How should they not say it? They are what they are. But my wife and I meet it together. She knows that my need of her drove me to fill it as I could. She need know no more."

"I suppose she does, like everyone else," said Nigel. "People think the past can be undone. Verena assumes that Malcolm will forget it. I would not, if I were he."

"You mean you would not, being yourself," said Malcolm. "No one would think it of you."

There was a silence that no one knew how to break, and Constance did what she could.

"I suppose Malcolm and Verena will be married soon?"

"Almost at once," said her cousin.

"And I suppose you will have a quiet wedding?"

"Not a wedding at all, simply a marriage," said Malcolm, remembering when someone else had said these words, and seeing that others remembered.

"And then you will have a honeymoon," said Constance, with her colour rising.

"How right you can be!"

"So she can, and so she often is," said Miles.

"And on your return you will have a house of your own?"

"I hope you are right again."

"There is room for them here," said Miles. "We will go back to our old ideas. They were our real ones."

"I think a separate home would be better, Father," said Constance.

"You should think again. It will be best to see everything as we always saw it. That is how we do see it. That is how it is."

Audrey said something in a low tone.

"What did you say?" said Miles.

"Nothing, Father. I only said that Mother used to be in favour of a separate house."

"And that is not nothing. That is everything. But everything is not what we can have in this world of ours. We cannot have it in this case. Malcolm and his wife will live in this house, as if things had gone as we meant. That is how they are going. Those that should not have happened, should not count to us. To me they do not count. They have come and gone as in a dream."

"It is good to have our dubious doings made into a dream," said Rudolf. "They are too often seen as real."

"I think this scene must really be a dream," said Nigel. "It could hardly be anything else."

"What are you talking about?" said Miles.

"I will tell you, Uncle. The way you rise to an occasion. It so seldom happens. I don't know how the phrase arose."

"Oh, I have risen to this one, have I?" said Miles, with a touch of complacence. "Well, I have tried to. It was for me to do it. I was the one who was shocked and stunned into stumbling forward almost unawares, because we have to go forward. So I was the one to resolve things and put them in their place. It seems to be a piling of everything on to one person. But there it was. And I have done my best with it."

"So Uncle is the hero of the story," said Rudolf. "It comes of taking matters into his own hands. That might help many of us."

"I wonder what Aunt Ellen thinks of him," said Nigel. "That is, I dare not wonder. I might come to a conclusion."

"Malcolm," said Constance, in a soft tone, "I think someone else is a hero."

Malcolm seemed not to hear.

"Ellen," said Eliza, coming up to her, "you are beyond all praise. And my nieces show a like spirit. It comes from you."

"I feel I am watching the scene. But I must begin to take my part. I have my home and my daughters; I have their need of me. It was a need that could not be filled, and I will not talk of another. How can I say anything about my poor husband?"

"Or I in another sense about my son? So we will say nothing. And neither of us knows what to say about the poor girl. So we will again say nothing."

"Goodbye, Eliza," said Miles. "We thank you for coming to be with us. It is a day we shall not forget."

"He hardly will," said Rudolf. "There is enough to stimulate recollection."

"He might," said Nigel. "He is going to forget a good deal."

"I am, Nigel," said Miles, in a deliberate tone. "I am going to tear a page of my life from the scroll of memory. It is a dim chapter, a story half-told. Or so it is to me."

"And to all of us," said Rudolf. "But it was moving to a climax. It would soon have been told."

"Perhaps we should try to see it as Father does," said Constance.

"No," said Ursula, "we do not owe him that."

"Father," said Constance, when her aunt had gone, "shall

we ever know who it was, who sent the money to Mother? I feel I want to know it more than anything."

"I am too thankful it was sent, to think any further. I am content to leave it. I should indeed be so."

"I am not. I find I cannot be. My mind keeps on returning to it. I cannot rest in ignorance."

"Come, come," said Miles, lifting his hand with a smile. "What about our obligation to respect his wish to be anonymous? Her wish I daresay. It may have been a woman. Anyhow he or she desired to remain unknown. And we must be content to be grateful and to probe no further. To do anything else would be a poor return."

"If the money ceases to come," said Malcolm, "we shall know it was someone who followed the course of things."

"I think we may infer that. And we must imagine no more. It will probably cease. That is the likely thing."

"We are so eager to show our gratitude," said Constance. "Or anyhow just to express it."

"Well, we must deny ourselves, or we shall not be showing it. We owe it to her to put the matter from our minds."

"You feel it was a woman, Uncle?" said Malcolm.

"Well, something seems to tell me so, though it is a voice I must not hear. A woman is on the whole a kinder creature than a man. She would feel for another woman."

"It is not your usual view of women, Mr. Mowbray," said Miss Gibbon.

"Oh, in deeper things it is. It is in the little, petty things that they are unfair to each other. And this is certainly not one of those. It is pleasant to hear your voice, Miss Gibbon. I wish we heard it oftener."

"You did not send the money to Mother, did you, Miss Gibbon?" said Constance.

"Of course she did not," said Miles. "She would not have it. I mean, she is not used to making moves of that kind. And she gave her what money she had. I admit the idea occurred to me, but I dismissed it."

"I should have taken it to her myself," said Miss Gibbon.

"Yes, you would, of course. That disposes of the question."

"It was a silly thought," said Constance. "But it must have been someone."

"Now, now!" said Miles, again raising his hand. "We shall have to say it was no one. Anyhow there is an end of it. Malcolm, my boy, shall we have a talk about your future? Ours is safe and settled, and we must turn our eyes to yours. Suppose you and I have a word in the library? And give the mother and daughters an hour to themselves? That seems to be due to them."

"Mother, can you rest without knowing who helped you in your need?" said Constance.

"I shall have no choice. It may transpire one day. Such things tend to do so. Not that I have met others like this. But a real secret is a rare thing."

"People must have their credit in the end," said Ursula.

"I do not mind how much credit they have," said Constance. "I am only too anxious to give it."

"As Father would agree. He is troubled by your want of scruple. Mother, are we to talk about him? He has given us the opportunity. He must have known we should use it."

"Yes, if we wish. Though there is nothing I need to know. Miss Gibbon told me everything. It was a hard time for you, and it promised harder ones. But it is in the past."

"The memory cannot be there. We have to carry it with us."

"Even Father must do that," said Constance. "Though I do not know why I should say 'even'."

"The rest of us do," said Audrey. "I can hardly believe any of it. Already it seems incredible. Father to marry Verena! Verena as our stepmother! It is the first time we have said it. When it was possible, it could not be said. And I am the one to say it. That brings it to an end."

"It is not necessary to say it now," said Constance.

"Yes, it is, to say it once. Then it is faced and said."

"Your poor father!" said Ellen. "I will not wonder what he suffered. Perhaps it was not much. Anyhow it was not for

148

long. And what is he feeling now? It is hard to say. In his way he has great courage."

"And great powers," said Ursula, "or anyhow strange ones. To think what these hours would have been, if they had been carried through by anyone else! He saves everyone in saving himself."

"And what he did was not actually wrong," said Constance.

"I think we must say it was," said her mother. "To Verena and to all of you, and more to Malcolm and to me. I am not the person to judge. But it is a simple question."

"In asking what he is feeling now, we are really asking how much he cared for Verena," said Constance, gently.

"We shall never know," said Ursula. "Or I suppose we never shall. There would be no way of telling us. Words would mean nothing. And how much did Verena care for him? We shall not know that either, or know better than we do. And the darkest figure is Malcolm."

"I think we may say he is an heroic figure too."

"Well, mind you do not say it."

"I hope I can sometime let him know that I think it."

"Well, I trust you will choose the way."

"It is not a thing that one would be clumsy about."

"It would be easy to appear to be so."

"Mother, if I may ask, what is your feeling towards Verena?"

"You know I have never seen her. But from what is said of her and what has happened, she is a person by herself. And that is not often said of anyone so young."

"I am glad Mother has said it," said Audrey. "No one could think she was like anyone else."

"I suppose no one is," said Constance.

"I am like almost everyone."

"But not like Father or Verena."

"So like Father that I almost understand everything. I feel I am just going to, and then it escapes."

"Mother, what do you feel about Malcolm and Verena's living here, when they are married?" said Constance.

"You know I think it unwise."

"And more unwise in view of what has been between Verena and Father?"

"I can hardly say. You know I am in the dark."

"Why do people—why do men feel so much for her? I don't want to be ungenerous, but I do not understand."

"She has youth and looks, and knows how to serve herself," said Ursula. "And the men in our life were those who came into hers. I do want to be ungenerous. And I have been so."

"Poor child! She was too young to be alone," said Ellen. "Now that is generous enough to become the opposite. The generosity is mine, and the pity is for her. And pity does not add to people."

"I am glad it does not," said Audrey.

"I am really sorry for her," said Constance.

"So am I," said Ursula. "So we really do not add to her. But I think we must add one thing. She has a sort of power."

"Yes, she has," said Audrey. "One could almost feel afraid of her."

"I suppose Father has given himself a strange name in the neighbourhood," said Constance. "I think we must say it."

"Well, we must know it," said Ursula. "And he has given us the same. And whether we say it or not, it will be said."

"Well, it is all settled," said Miles, returning to the room. "The marriage is to be as soon as possible, as quiet as possible, and as much else as is possible. They will have a short honeymoon, and then return to this house. Verena will not come here until it is over. And then she will settle down in the home where she will one day be mistress. And you need not all look at me, and then in that way at each other. I could never open my mouth, if I thought if my words were awkward, or aroused embarrassing memories. Of course everything I say must be of that kind, and could not be said, if I allowed myself to think. You can see a matter as it is. I hope none of you will ever be in a difficult place. For I do not know how you would manage in it."

"Not as well as you do, Father," said Ursula. "You are the character of the story."

"Character of it? Well, I suppose I am in a way. The demand has been on me. Everyone else has been able to be generous and heroic. And I have been ridiculous and pitiful and a sort of spectacle and butt. And doing more all the time than anyone else, and facing more into the bargain! Indeed no one else doing or facing anything! It has been a test on a large scale. It has been a hard thing to rise to it. I doubt if anyone has faced a greater one, or one as penetrating and painful. I did not dare to think what it was. I just went through it. I suppose that is what people did, when they went to the scaffold or the stake. And they had admiration to support them, and I had not anything. I had not indeed. You should have seen your row of faces. And those two boys of Eliza's behaving as if they had come to gape at a spectacle! And all I had done was to try to mend my life, when it was broken through no fault of my own. Well, now it is whole again, and we can forget what is past. Not that I can ever forget it. And you will remember it in another way. Oh, I don't doubt that you will. Ellen, my wife, you are tired and troubled. And no one has seen it but your husband. And I don't feel so very different. We will go and care for each other."

"I have always thought self-praise had too little justice," said Ursula.

"It has," said Audrey. "It is a great recommendation."

CHAPTER XII

"WELCOME, MY BOY, welcome to your home. Welcome to you both. Here is our household as we ought to have it, as it should have been. We put the seal on our true life, on our settled future. Welcome to both of you again."

Miles used the tone of an uncle to a nephew and niece.

Verena glanced into his face as she withdrew from his greeting, and a faint smile came to her lips. He appeared not to see it, and moved aside for his wife.

"Now, here is the best welcome of all, the one that should have come first, that counts the most! Ah, I have looked for this moment."

Verena just cast her eyes over Ellen.

"We meet for the first time," she said, in a simply conventional tone, offering her hand.

"Well, we all have to do that," said Miles. "There is a first time to everything. Now here is our family complete. It is good to see you all together. I take a pride in my four daughters. We shall be a happy family round the tea table."

"That is a rash word," said Audrey. "I suppose this is the way to do it. But could it not have been left undone?"

"The moment had to be got through," said Constance.

"It could surely have been omitted. It would have passed by itself."

"Perhaps not with any success," said Ursula. "Moments seem to need some help. Or they seem to need Father's. And he can be relied on to give it."

Verena walked into the dining-room, and paused at her former seat on Miles's right, giving him a different smile.

"That is Ursula's place, Verena," said Constance. "There is another set for you."

Verena glanced at her and again at Miles, and remained standing.

"We can surely sit anywhere at an oval table," said Malcolm. "No place is different from another."

"We each have our own," said Miles. "But there is room and to spare for the new one. As you say, a table like this renders all things equal."

"I displaced Ursula when I returned," said Ellen, taking her own seat opposite her husband.

"No, we left your place empty, Mother," said Constance. "It was yours, and could never be anything else to us."

Miles looked at the window and tapped his foot on the carpet.

"Well, no seat will be empty now. And we shall all be accommodated."

"I do not know which is mine," said Verena, still waiting uncertainly.

"We will all take our own," said Ursula. "And that will simplify your problem, indeed solve it."

"The extra one," said Malcolm. "The furthest on Aunt Ellen's right; the one by mine."

"Well, I will move it to fill up the circle. And sit on Miles's left hand instead of his right."

"How did you all sit, when I was away?" said Ellen. "Did you not have your usual seats?"

"We sat as we do now, Mother. But all a place further from Father," said Constance, looking at nothing. "So that the seat on his right hand was free."

"Oh, no one can assign seats at a table like this," said Miles. "Are we not to have any tea? Ellen, my dear, that silver teapot is heavy for you. Could Ursula manage it?"

"I suppose she did, when I was away. And I did before I went. And I am still equal to it."

"I remember you thought I should not be," said Verena to Miles. "It needs a stronger wrist than mine."

"Well, you will not have to be," said Malcolm.

"Not for a while," said Miles. "The time will come one day."

"I hope not for many years, Uncle."

"Thank you, my boy, I am in no hurry for it. I trust no one else is."

"I am not, Father," said Constance, smiling.

"Are we all to give the assurance?" said Ursula.

"I am sure we can all do so," said Constance.

"My Audrey, am I not to hear your voice? It is more silent than it used to be."

"You can hardly need to hear it at the moment, Father."

"In a family like this a woman has no place," said Verena, without raising her eyes. "It depends on the man she has married."

"There is one woman who has one," said Miles, looking at Ellen. "The first place in the house, the place of the wife and mother. No other comes up to it."

"Well, that is what I mean. It does not depend on herself."

"You hardly seem to mean much," said Malcolm.

"How do you like your tea, Verena?" said Constance. "My mother is waiting to know."

"Your father could have told her."

"I think you can tell me yourself," said Ellen, smiling.

"I am not used to saying that sort of thing in this house."

"I think you must tell me this once. It can be the first and last time."

Verena made no answer and looked at Miles.

"Oh, I do not know," he said, withdrawing his eyes. "It is not the kind of thing I remember."

"I think you do know."

Miles seemed not to hear, and looked again at his wife.

"Malcolm, relieve your aunt of that teapot. It is too much for her."

Malcolm took the pot from Ellen, and supplied his cousins.

"When is my turn?" said Verena, in a light tone.

"When you say what you want. I do not know. You always pour out the tea yourself."

"As I have said, Miles can tell you."

"Well, I cannot," said the latter. "And why should I

be able to? I have never thought about it. I am not a woman."

"Were you one, when you and I had tea together?"

"Well, I suppose you were, and still are. The tea is your province. It is not a thing I should notice."

"You seemed to notice everything," said Verena, in a lower tone.

"Well, I did not. I am not observant of details."

"You did not think this was a detail."

"Well, the rest of us do," said Malcolm. "And it will be treated as one. I will pour out my own tea."

"And pour out Miles's too. I can tell you how he has it."

"He can tell me himself. And you had better call him 'Uncle Miles', as I do."

"No I had not. How could I? It would be like playing a part."

"Yes, I think it would be more suitable, Verena," said Constance.

"Had you not better think again? Think a moment longer."

"I have thought. And that is my conclusion. And would you not be more comfortable, doing so?"

"I hope you will do so, when I am here, Verena," said Ellen, resuming the teapot to cover her words.

"Well, I need not call him anything, unless we are alone."

"You will not be alone," said Audrey. "Father will either be with Mother or in the library."

"Well, I shall sometimes be there."

"No, the library is sacred to Malcolm and me and our duty," said Miles, shaking his head and using a resigned tone.

"It used to be sacred in another way," said Verena.

"Well, now everything has settled again, the old obligations return."

"The life will not suit you very well."

"Father is looking better and younger than he has for some time," said Constance.

"He looks as he did when I was here before. I suppose the time after that was too much for him."

"He did not look as happy and well as he does now."

"Well, you and I would not see him in the same way."

"What rooms are we to have, Uncle?" said Malcolm.

"That is a question for your aunt to answer."

"The two at the end of the small passage," said Ellen. "Those your uncle and I had, when we were first married, and lived here with his parents."

"A west room with a little dressing-room?" said Verena.

"Yes, I hope you will like them. They were the only ones that were free."

"I daresay they are good enough for those," said Verena, smiling.

"Oh, come, they are good enough in themselves," said Miles. "They are the natural ones for you to have. Those we had in your position."

"There are really no others," said Ellen. "All the rest are needed."

"Most things are," said Verena, "in the sense of being wanted by somebody."

"I could change my room, if it served any purpose, Mother," said Constance.

"It hardly does. They need two adjoining rooms."

"Mine is next to Constance's," said Ursula. "But I will not offer to relinquish it. I am happy in it myself."

"Sensibly said," said Miles, twirling his moustache and giving a little laugh.

"The matter is settled," said Malcolm. "And they are the rooms we should expect to have."

"It has settled itself," said Ellen. "The house is only what it is. I have never wanted it different."

"I would not have a stick or a stone changed," said Miles, more loudly. "It is my home, the home of my forefathers, the home of those who come after me. I love every scar and crack on it."

"Then you can love those rooms," said Verena. "I saw them when you showed me over the house."

"I can and do. They are a part of it."

"I used to have the large, spare room opposite to yours."

"Well, that is still the large, spare room," said Constance, "and has to remain so."

"And it has no dressing-room," said Audrey.

"The dressing-room need not be next door," said Verena, looking at Miles, and changing her tone as he was silent. "How quickly everything can become different!"

"Of course I am different since my life was restored to me," he said, using a resolute note and looking at no one. "Or rather I can be my old self again."

"You seem to me an unchangeable person, Father," said Constance. "Now is that shallow or deep?"

"It is anyhow rash," said Ursula to Malcolm. "Especially as it has its truth."

"Well, am I to have any tea?" said Verena.

"When we know how you like it," said Constance.

"Ursula must know. She has often poured it out."

"You must know yourself," said the latter. "And my mother is pouring it out to-day. It would be natural for you to tell her."

"Oh, let me have it anyhow."

Ellen filled a cup, and passed milk and sugar with it.

"Now you remember how I have it," said Verena, taking a very little of each and looking at Miles.

"Oh, it will not remain in my head. I dislike a burdened memory."

"It used not to be a burden."

"It would have been, if my mind had held it. Ellen, my dear, your own cup came late. It could not have been a good one. We will ring for some more tea."

"Mine was last of all," said Verena, looking at her cup. "And it does not make for goodness."

"Whose fault was it, that it was last?" said Constance, lightly.

"Well, Verena's can be first this time," said Ellen, as fresh tea was brought.

"No, take your own first, my love," said Miles, leaning forward. "Do not have it after the young ones. It is the wrong order."

"It is the usual one," said Ellen, as she filled Verena's cup.

"Now yours, Mother," said Constance. "And then we will follow in turn."

"The mistress of the house is used to coming last," said Verena. "She expects it in her place."

"Well, in yours you come first," said Ursula. "You are the one of us nearest to a guest. All positions have their advantages."

"And some have other things."

"Well, of course they do. The first shall be last and the last first," said Miles, not quite sure of his meaning.

"It seems to be so," said Verena, looking down.

"You are feeling you are not my real daughter," said Miles, in a tone of sympathy. "But you will come to be one, as Malcolm becomes more my son. There will be less and less difference."

"I could never feel I was your daughter," said Verena, in a lower tone. "There must always be the difference. May I have some sugar, Mrs. Mowbray? The least of all the lumps."

"Will you not call me 'Aunt Ellen', as Malcolm does?"

"Well, but Malcolm and I have a different past."

"But the same present. And that is what we are concerned with."

"I cannot only think of one time in my life. And the one that is most strange to me. All this seems to me unnatural. I do not think of you as my aunt."

"You will come to," said Miles, in a full tone. "With every day you will get nearer to it. We can see you making a beginning. And we respect you for it. We admire your power to adapt yourself. You are young and supple, and change is natural to you."

"I do not think it is. People judge others by themselves. It does not seem to depend on youth."

There was the sound of the front door, and Miles was able to turn his head.

"So you wonder who it is, Uncle?" said Malcolm. "The truth is too consistent to be probable."

"Oh, we ought to have asked them!" said Constance.

"It does not matter," said her father. "What difference does it make? The result would be the same."

"Not quite, Miles. We are asked or we are not. And it does make a difference. But I felt I might come and welcome a son and daughter, who really belong to me more than to you. We waited until we thought tea would be over. So I hope we are not disturbing it?"

"It is over, Aunt Eliza," said Constance. "But may we not have some more for you?"

"Pray let us, Eliza," said Miles. "We should choose to do so. It is our wish. We ask you to grant it."

"No, no, we knew we were not expected. We had it before we came. We are here to greet our travellers and see them in their new home. You know I have had them both in mine. And that adds to my feeling."

"It is not a new home for Malcolm," said Constance.

"And hardly for Verena," said Audrey, in a low tone, "or only in another sense."

"What did you say, my dear?" said Eliza.

"Oh, nothing, nothing that had any meaning."

"Come, words always mean something," said Miles. "What did you say?"

"She said it was hardly a new home for me either," said Verena. "Why should she not say it?"

"It is surely better not to return to that other time," said Constance.

"It was a phantom time," said Miles, on an almost exasperated note. "Surely we can leave it behind."

"It did not seem to be," said Verena, looking into his face. "And we may find that it was not."

"Have you told your new family the news that Malcolm wrote to me?" said Eliza. "It was my right to know it first, as I was most concerned. But I am eager to share it. Do they know I am to be a grandmother? And do they think I can fill the part? I am resolving to do my best in it."

"No, Eliza, we have not been told," said Miles. "We thank you indeed for telling us. And we congratulate you and them, and indeed ourselves, from our hearts. It is great news to all of us, to my wife and daughters and to me. And to you as much as any of us."

"To me the most of all. Malcolm is my son."

"It opens up the future and teaches us to look forward," said Constance, lowering her tone as she ended. "And I hope it will help us to cease looking back, and help someone else to do so."

"Which do you want, Verena, a son or a daughter?" said Miss Gibbon.

"I would much rather have a son."

"Be careful," said Constance. "You may have a daughter."

"Well, she cannot overhear at this stage," said Nigel.

"Ah, ha! No, she can't," said Miles. "But she might come to know it. What a thing to say for the first word you utter! I hardly knew you were here."

"We were told to be seen and not heard," said Rudolf. "And we do not seem even to have achieved the first."

"If I have a son, he cannot live here," said Verena. "He must be brought up in a house where his mother is mistress."

"Then I hope you will not have one," said Miles, using an easy tone. "Because there is no such house."

"How Uncle has altered his way of talking to Verena!" said Nigel.

"He has not altered it. He has transferred it to Aunt Ellen. He had already transferred it from her."

"Now tell us what it is, Rudolf," said Miles, with a sigh.

"Oh, nothing, Uncle. It only concerned Nigel and me."

"I suppose that is not the truth. I doubt if you can speak it."

"That is a hard accusation, Father," said Constance.

"Hard or not, it might be a frequent one. And I expect there was some hidden meaning."

"Then I hope it will remain hidden," said Ursula. "This had to be a strange occasion. But need it be more so than it must? I wonder if there has ever been a similar one."

"Well, I daresay not," said Miles, with a faint laugh and a glance towards his wife. "I suppose it is unique and will leave its own memory. But it had to come. And we are getting through it."

"I think it must cease to be what it is," said Ellen, turning and speaking quietly. "There has been no need. And there must not be another. And I shall not say it again."

"Indeed you will not," said Miles, in an emphatic, rather empty tone. "Indeed you shall not. You have spoken, and that is enough."

"It must be good to be Aunt Ellen and have absolute power," said Nigel.

"Yes, it must," said Verena.

"I am not so sure," said Rudolf. "People who have power seem to need it."

"There could not be a more benevolent rule," said Miss Gibbon.

"There could not," said Miles, in the same tone. "It is the most selfless, generous sway that ever governed a household. I know nothing that compares to it."

"Having been balked of the opportunity to make comparisons," said Nigel.

"Now I shall not ask you what it was. No doubt you expect me to. It is your way of exhibiting yourself."

"I am ashamed of them," said Eliza. "Will you both be silent?"

"I have been ashamed of Verena," said Constance to Ursula.

"She is in a difficult place. But if only she would remain there! We did not foresee the view she would take of it."

"Did she expect to be a sort of second mistress of the house?" said Audrey.

"She has not made the necessary transition," said Constance. "It must have been hard for poor Mother to say what she did."

"But it was good to hear it said."

"I am afraid we resent it in Verena that she meant to be our stepmother."

"We cannot be expected to appreciate it," said Ursula. "And she scarcely seems to have given up the idea."

"It is difficult to see the future."

"Well, the present should be enough."

"So it should," said Miles, half-hearing. "It is all we should ask. And I would ask no more. I live in the present. I give myself up to the present. I trust myself to it. I should be an ingrate, if I did not. There is no sense in dwelling on a past that can give us nothing more. And we must leave the future. It can take care of itself. Or anyhow we cannot alter it."

"The last is not quite true, Father," said Constance.

"There is always meaning in the past," said Verena. "We live in it, because it is itself alive."

"Oh, come, at your age!" said Miles. "Your time is in the future."

"There is no such difference. Nothing ever dies."

"Come, do not talk like a greybeard. Everything dies day by day. Otherwise we could not live."

"If that were true, we never should have lived."

"There is something in what Verena says," said Constance.

"It is true that the past has not died," said Malcolm.

"Well, some things remain, the vital things," said Miles. "But I thank God that mine are still with me. I do not have to look back for them."

"I have always looked back," said Verena. "I believe all thinking people do."

"Always! What can that mean at your age?"

"Words have the same meaning at any age."

"No, that can hardly be true. Not words like 'always'."

"Can Verena talk to no one but Father?" said Constance.

"One would almost have thought she would avoid talking to him."

"What we may have thought has ceased to have any meaning," said Audrey.

"What? What is that?" said Miles.

"Father, you must let people speak," said Constance, "without wanting them to repeat everything they say."

"Well, I can let you do so. I don't suspect you of anything. It is your cousins who keep me on tenterhooks all the time."

"Aunt Eliza is silent," said Constance. "She would be more help, if she talked in her usual way."

"I think it is Mother who troubles her," said Audrey. "She watches her all the time."

"And I do not wonder," said Ursula. "One sees what someone meant, when he thanked the gods that dead men rise up never."

"Well, I would not do that," said Miles. "I thank them for a different thing. I am one of the rare people who have had it happen."

"So Father has been singled out," said Audrey. "And it is natural that he should be."

"It was Swinburne who wrote the words," said Constance.

"Well, Swinburne is wrong as far as I am concerned," said Miles.

"It was a wise thing to say," said Verena.

"No, no, it was not. It was written for effect, and to sound wise by being unexpected. I don't say it has no truth."

"It must either have the whole truth or none."

"Is that so? I do not follow. I shall have another daughter who bewilders me."

"Uncle is good at manipulating relationships," said Nigel.

"What is that? No, you need not say. I am beginning to see you as you are. You are a person apart from me. I hardly feel you are my nephew."

"What relation will you arrange for me to be?"

"Oh, I do not know. I would not have you for a son."

"If he would, he could have you for one," said Rudolf.

163

"What is that?" said Miles. "What are you laughing at, Eliza? I don't see any joke. No, pray do not leave us, Miss Gibbon. You are one of us. Why, you and my wife are like sisters. Now what is there laughable in that?"

"Uncle uses his gifts unconsciously." said Nigel. "That shows they go deep."

"Well, I daresay I do," said Miles. "If they involved an effort, they would not be gifts. I have never been one of those people who struggle and moil through life. What I do must be done easily. I am the opposite of your father. I sometimes can hardly believe I am his brother."

"Then why not be something else?"

"We must be going, Ellen," said Eliza. "I wish we could do something for you. It is the thing I would choose of all others. Things are hardly as I hoped and thought. But if you had foreseen them, you would still have chosen to return."

"Yes, I am not so different from other people. I wish I had chosen sooner. And there are things I feel I may put right. I am as little different as that."

Malcolm spoke as soon as his mother had gone.

"May Verena go to her room, Aunt Ellen? She is cold and tired."

"She can hardly be cold near that great fire," said Constance.

"It is because she is cold that she is near it."

"Tired I am sure she is," said Ellen. "You know the rooms, and can take her to them."

"I know them," said Verena. "They were used as odd spare rooms."

"We did not have guests while you were here," said Constance.

"No, but that is how we should have used them."

"Your aunt and I had them in your exact position," said Miles. "That was not using them in that way."

"No, it was making them fill another breach. And now they are to fill a third. They do their workaday part."

Miles took up the paper and did not reply, and Ellen followed the couple upstairs.

"Well, cannot you even enter the rooms?" she said, as she found them on the threshold.

"We are trying to get to know them in their new character," said Verena.

"I have known them and lived with them in it. It is not a hard thing to do. I have to ask you something harder."

"What do you mean?" said Verena at once.

"I think I need scarcely tell you."

"You had better put it into words."

"No, they would always be remembered."

"Do you mean these to be forgotten?"

"Not until they have done their work. Then I hope they will be."

"You want me to forget a chapter of my life."

"No, only not to appear to remember it."

"I am afraid of hurting Miles."

"You can hardly be so any longer."

"It is such a changed world. I cannot see how I am to live in it."

"You must have known it would have changed."

"To me it will be like the world before it did so," said Malcolm.

"And it should be to me," said Ellen. "And I am asking Verena to let it be."

"It is asking too much," said Verena. "We cannot undo the past."

"You must see it has lost its meaning."

"That is not to say it never had it. Nothing can be undone."

"It means that it did not go deep."

"It went as deep as anything else," said Verena, with tears in her voice. "There are things in your life that do not go deep. I have seen you facing and accepting them. I can observe as much as you can. Why should I be so different?"

Ellen turned and left the room, and Verena flung herself on the bed and broke into weeping.

"Come, this can do nothing," said Malcolm. "She is right, and you can only obey. It is the one thing that will serve you."

"She would always be right. I do not dare to disobey. She has the power. But things are so easy for people who have the power and must be obeyed. I wish I could make something hard for her, just one thing."

"You know you have done so. And she has had many things hard."

"She says they have lost their meaning. I wish I could bring it home to her, make her acknowledge it. If I could do just that, it would be different. Then I could try to accept her as what you say she is."

"She will not bear anything. And I had better say now, if not again, that I will not either."

"No one is on my side. I must do what I can for myself."

"There is nothing you can do, of good to yourself or harm to her. And you cannot mean to do her harm."

Verena rose and went to the window.

"There may be something," she said.

At dinner everyone was in an easier mood. The new life seemed to be on foot, and it was possible to accept it. Conventions were followed, and Verena's manner to both Miles and Ellen was less tense and unnatural. She seemed to be facing the future and to realise the vanity of opposing it. Miles was easy and paternal, feeling and responding to the change.

"Well, there are questions ahead of us. They will be upon us sooner than we think. That is a way they have. What rooms are to be the nurseries?"

"Those that have always been," said Constance. "Those that were yours and ours."

"And should be my grandchildren's. I cannot help wishing they were to be. I don't know why it came over me, but I felt a sudden desire to see my descendants in my home. And if I have them, they will be in the homes of others. Well, it is late to regret it. I must be grateful for what I have."

"You and I both have a wish unsatisfied, Father," said Constance. "You cannot be content without a grandson to follow you. And I cannot be, without knowing who it was, who helped Mother in her need. We both find it hard to be reconciled."

"You may both have your wish in the end," said Verena.

"We can neither of us have it," said Miles.

"The money has ceased to come," said Audrey. "So it must be someone who knows about everything."

"We have come to that conclusion before. We can get no further."

"It seems we might be able to follow it up," said Constance. "It might not be impossible to get on the tracks."

"Follow it up! Get on the tracks!" said Miles. "What would she say to it? We can surely respect the wish of someone who has served us. There should not be any question."

"I am sure it was a man," said Verena.

"How can you be sure?" said Constance.

"I can only say that I am."

"Why not be sure who it was?" said Malcolm.

"Well, there are reasons," said his wife.

"Mother, what was the postmark on the envelopes?" said Constance. "How strange that we did not think of that before!"

"Oh, I thought of it," said Miles. "How could I not? But I was unwilling to pry. And a postmark could prove nothing."

"It was that of a village between that one and this. It gave no clue," said Ellen. "As far as I can say, we do not know anyone there."

"Someone might have had it posted there," said Ursula.

"Yes, that is obvious," said Miles. "That is why it can have no meaning."

"We can get no further," said Malcolm. "So I suppose we shall never leave the question."

"Indeed we shall. We shall leave it now. This is no way to treat a woman to whom we owe so much, to pursue what she meant to be hidden."

"I suppose it must emerge in time," said Verena.

"How can it? It would have done so by now, if prying and probing could help it. I am glad she cannot know how we hunt and hound her. I feel quite ashamed of being a party to it."

"You surely need not feel that, Father," said Constance.

"Oh, well, I should like to know as much as any of you. More I daresay, as I am most deeply concerned. But for me it is not a matter for mere curiosity, for the very reason that it goes so deep."

"Why should curiosity be mere?" said Malcolm. "And always concerned with the surface? It is not the truth."

"It goes deeper than many feelings," said Audrey. "It is because it demands something instead of giving it."

"The end can only come with the discovery," said Verena.

"Then it will never come," said Miles.

"Women are curious, Mr. Mowbray," said Miss Gibbon. "It is known to be their nature."

"They are other things as well," said Constance. "Or there would not have been one to help Mother."

"Neither would there," said Miles, with a sigh. "Neither would there. And we are thankful that there was. Let us say it, as we leave the subject for ever. 'God bless her.' And now I think any further word would be bathos."

"What a courageous thing to say, when you have made a speech!" said Audrey.

"Why, I don't see anything about it that needed courage."

"It must be held to suggest a change of subject," said Malcolm.

"We should have asked Aunt Eliza to be with us this afternoon," said Constance, following the suggestion. "It is a matter where we must turn over a new leaf."

"The occasions are over," said Malcolm.

"There will be others," said Verena.

"I cannot imagine any equal to those we have had."

"I can. A family history goes on."

"There will be trivial ones," said Miles. "And we must

remember to ask her. Malcolm, shall we say it is your province?"

"I am too used to following her suggestions to think of making any. And she is incapable of coming alone."

"Yes, without those boys," said his uncle with a frown. "It puts me out of sorts to think of them."

"I daresay they will improve, as they get older," said Constance.

"I like them as they are," said Verena.

"Yes, I do not want them changed," said Ellen, smiling.

"Well, I will not either, if you both feel it," said Miles, as if welcoming the agreement.

"I think we all look tired," said Constance, looking round.

"I am sure I feel so," said her father. "And I suppose there is reason. And you are tired, my Ellen. And so are our four dear girls. It seems a long time since the morning."

"And since the afternoon," said Verena. "We did not reach the house until five."

"Yes, it has been a time by itself. We can see it as it is, as we understand each other. And it will leave no trace. If we have been through fire and water, we have come out un-scathed. If virtue has gone out of us, we have only to rest and recover. I will set the example and go upstairs. Ellen, you will follow me. Good-night, all my dear ones. Good-night, Malcolm, my boy. We shall begin a new life tomorrow."

"I will go up too," said Verena. "Malcolm, you will give me time. A woman needs longer than a man. You could go and find something to read."

Malcolm went into the library, and the mother and daughters were together.

"Mother, we are hardly ever alone with you now," said Constance.

"We have not been to-day," said Ursula. "And it is indeed a stretch of time. I can hardly remember the beginning. We seem at the end of experience. So we may hope there is to be a change."

"There must be," said Ellen. "It is one of us who makes the

trouble. And she must be fairer to us all. I will not see you with a spoiled home."

"When for a time we hardly had one," said Audrey.

"When it has been given back to you. And Malcolm must not suffer anything. His endurance may break down."

"And so may yours," said Ursula.

"Yes, I know I have less than I had."

"And there is more demand on it."

"At the moment. But it must cease."

Ellen went upstairs before her daughters, and came upon Miles and Verena talking outside her door. They appeared undisturbed when they saw her, and moved aside for her to pass. She bade good-night to Verena and entered the room, signing to her husband to follow.

"What had Verena to say to you?" she said at once, as if the time for silence could be accepted as past.

"Something about the coming child. She wants me to treat it as my grandchild. I am afraid I was rather unthinking in what I said at dinner. I promised that you and I would both do our best. I knew I might speak of us as one. We will try to welcome it, as if it were our own. I see it is the right thing to do."

"And Verena herself must do the right things."

"Yes, I dropped a hint of that too," said Miles.

CHAPTER XIII

"FATHER, WE ARE on the forbidden subject," said Constance, as Miles came to breakfast a few days later. "Something is always giving rise to it. Malcolm was working, and wanted some registered envelopes. And it was in one of those that the money came to Mother. So the discussion arose again from the beginning."

"Well, it is forbidden, as you say," said her father, taking up a letter. "You must learn to leave it alone."

"It does not seem so easy."

"Well, make a little effort then. That will not hurt you."

"Effort hurts everyone," said Audrey. "So the subject must tend to return."

"Until you get at the truth," said Verena. "And you will do that one day."

Miles made an exasperated gesture without raising his eyes.

"I am not going to say it again. Why should I waste my words? I can leave that to all of you. I use mine with a purpose. If Malcolm wants registered envelopes, I can let him have them."

"There are some in your desk," said Verena, "or there used to be. I remember the arrangement of it."

"Then they are there still. I do not use them. I will find them and give them to him."

"I will fetch them for you," said Verena, rising.

"No, no!" said Miles, looking up and lifting his hand. "Leave them where they are. I do not like my desk tampered with. It means I cannot put my hand on anything. No man can tolerate a woman's meddling with his papers. I should not interfere with anything of hers."

"You draw too hard and fast a line, Father," said Constance. "There is no definite division."

"Well, I need not draw one at all. My desk will remain untouched by any human hand."

"What would you call mine?" said Verena. "You asked me to put it in order. Am I below the human level or above it?"

"Which do you think?" said Audrey.

"I was not left to decide."

"You do not use the desk much, do you, Father?" said Constance.

"I put it to my own purposes. What do you know about it?"

"All that is to be known," said Ursula to Malcolm. "But there is no reason why it should not remain untouched. It is its usual state."

"You can get those envelopes at the post office," said Audrey.

"Well, of course," said her father. "They are sold for the purpose of registering. What would you suppose?"

"I will get them from the desk myself," said Malcolm.

"No, you will not," said his uncle. "Will you stop talking about my desk? Can't you hear what I say?"

"I am not a woman, Uncle."

"You might be, for the way you pursue a point to its death. Why cannot you leave it? What does it matter who gets the envelopes?"

"That was my feeling. I should have thought it did not matter."

"And neither does it. So we will not talk as if it did. We will leave the subject."

"There is the newsboy's bell," said Constance. "Will Everard bring the papers? He often does not hear."

"I will go and get them," said Verena. "He does not seem to be coming."

"Cannot Malcolm go?" said Miles. "Oh, well, thank you, Verena."

"Verena is very considerate," said Constance. "And she seems in a happier mood. She is settling down."

"There is no need to talk of her as if she were an accepted problem," said Malcolm.

"It is enough to know it," murmured Audrey.

"Why, what is the harm in that?" said Miles. "Constance meant very well. I had noticed the change myself. Had not you, Ellen?"

"I had noticed something," said his wife.

Verena returned with the papers and some of the envelopes, and laid them on the table.

"Well, I did it all at once. You were agreed that it did not matter. So I acted as if it did not."

"Give the envelopes to me," said Miles, holding out his hand, with his eyes on them.

"It is Malcolm who wants them. I hope I have brought enough."

She had brought one too many.

"There is one that is addressed," said Ursula. "Addressed to Mother like those that were sent with the money! And in the same printed hand. Did Mother bring the last one home with her?"

"No, I had opened the last," said Ellen. "It was almost time for another. I suppose this is it. I suppose it was sent here. My friend must have known I had returned. How did it get in the desk? Where exactly was it, Verena?"

"Oh, I suppose with the others. I did not see."

Miles looked in front of him, with a faint hum coming from his lips.

"It has no stamp or postmark," said Ursula. "It has not been through the post! Did someone put it in the desk, meaning to post it?"

There was a pause.

"Or knowing there was no need to post it," said Malcolm.

Miles drew his brows together, as if in some preoccupation, and rocked himself to and fro.

"So someone here sent the money," said Audrey. "And it was not Miss Gibbon."

Miles turned his eyes on the latter, almost as if in appeal.

"Father, was it you who sent it?" said Constance, in a deep tone.

"Was it I? Well," said Miles, still with his brows contracted, and still just rocking to and fro; "well, I could not let your mother starve, could I?"

"Did you know she was alive, and where she was?" said Ursula. "Why did you not tell us?"

"My good girl," said Miles, speaking as though coming out of a reverie, and turning slowly to her, "what was I to do? What would you have done? Answer me that, if you can."

"Tell us the whole, Father," said Constance. "Do not leave it to come out by stages. They say that to know all is to forgive all. And we will hope it will be so in this case."

"Why should you hope anything? What is it to do with you? You have no understanding of the matter, no power to understand it."

"We had the power to suffer from it," said Ursula. "And you can try to help our understanding. It will need the help."

"I thought your mother was dead," said Miles, in a deliberate, even tone, as if to make it as easy as he could for them. "You know we all thought it. Or I suppose you know. You cannot have forgotten that. And then I came upon something addressed to her by Miss Gibbon, and knew she was alive. And the matter stood as it did. She was supposed to be dead. I was engaged to be married. Both were accepted. Both had had their results. What was I to do? I did not know any more than she did. You know she did not know. Any more than Miss Gibbon did. You know she did not know either. And no one could have told us. Certainly you could not. So you need not look at me with accusing eyes, as if I ought to have faced the truth, when the truth was impossible, and there was nothing possible about anything. There was no hint of help anywhere. There was no precedent to follow. I sent the money by way of marking time. I had to see your mother was provided for, hadn't I? I suppose you see that? And I suppose you see nothing wrong about it? And I arranged for Miss Gibbon to deal with her things, and to come and go as she wished. What more could I do? It was an unbelievable state of matters. No one could have dealt with it."

"You could have gone to Mother and brought her back," said Audrey.

"And she could have come to me. And we neither of us did so. That means it was all too much for us. How could it have been anything else? Was it my fault that she did not return to me? Or hers that I could not resolve to go to her, and tell her what had befallen me in my solitude? I had always depended on her in the problems of life. I was not equal to facing such a one alone. She is a stronger person than I am, as you will all agree. You are the last people to complain of my dependence on her. It was Miss Gibbon who brought things to a pass, and gave us back our lives and each other. It cannot be said too often that she is our good friend."

"Would you have gone on for ever, knowing what you did?"

"For ever? I told you I was marking time. Don't you listen to a word I say? No wonder you get a wrong impression of me."

"You were going to marry Verena in a week."

"How do you know what I was going to do? How do I know? How can anyone know?"

"We cannot help knowing that you meant your plans to be carried out, Father," said Constance.

"Well, stop asking questions, if you cannot help knowing. You can answer them better than I can."

"Things would have grown more difficult with every day."

"That is what they did," said Miles, with open grimness. "And with every day."

"Father, I must say it," said Constance. "At some time it will have to be said. It had better be at once. You seemed happy and satisfied as things were, as they were held to be."

"Happy! With this on my mind!" said Miles, as if to himself.

"He was happy and satisfied," said Verena.

"Verena, did you know the envelope was in the desk?" said Ursula. "Did you bring it on purpose?"

"If I say I did not, you will not believe me."

"If you say you did, we will."

"Yes, I knew it was there. I knew your father had put it there. I saw him hide it on the day when your mother returned. And when I returned myself, I looked at it and saw what it was. You say that truth is best, and you need not complain of having it. And now you have the whole truth about everything, you need not complain at all. And I do not think you will."

"My desk!" said Miles. "If only it had not been touched! If only my word had been followed!"

"Father, at this moment!" said Constance.

"This is the moment that would have been avoided. Your mother would have been spared it. And I should have been spared it myself. And I think it is time I was spared something. I think it is indeed."

"There have been other moments," said Ursula. "This one gives them their meaning. We have to go back and see them with it."

"It will be a painful course, Father," said Constance. "And there are many of them. You did not help the trouble by waiting, when every hour added to it."

"And do I forget those hours? Who else should remember them? They had me in their power. I was carried on by them."

"Why did you not destroy the envelope?" said Malcolm.

"I meant to and put it off," said Miles, with truth in his tone. "Then I came to shrink from the sight of it. I felt I could not touch it. It seemed to have a life of its own."

"And has had one," said Ursula.

"Can we help you with it now, Father?" said Constance, quietly.

Miles passed her the envelope, keeping his eyes from it. She opened it, gave him the notes and put it on the fire. He handed the money to his wife, as though it were hers, and looked away.

"Father, did you mean it to go on for ever?" said Audrey.

"It could not have done so," said Constance.

"I suppose not," said Miles. "I suppose I knew that in my heart."

"That is what he meant," said Verena. "That is how he wished it to be. That is how it should have been."

At these words the sisters looked at their mother, somehow recalled by them to her silence.

"I ought to have come home at once," she said. "I should have come as soon as I could. I did not know what to do. But I should have known. The delay did no good, and could not have done any. I can hardly say why I waited. I thought I meant to leave your father to his life. But I could hardly have meant it. I was ill, and the truth was too much for me."

"The delay had no reason," said Verena. "You could not have intended it for anything else. You were willing to return, when Malcolm came for you."

"She was," said Miles. "And suppose she had not been! Well, we need not imagine it. She was willing."

"Father," said Constance, "there is one more thing. It is better to get it behind. When you said you felt sure that the giver of the money was a woman, what was in your mind? I hope it is not a callous question. It is one that has to come."

"I am glad it is both," muttered Malcolm.

"In my mind?" said Miles, leaning back and using a dreamy tone, but with his eyes narrowing on his daughter. "What was in it, do you say? What gave me the idea that a woman served my wife? What made the picture in my thought? Who was it, do you mean? Surely we see her before us in our good friend, Miss Gibbon. She it was, who gave your mother what help she could, and was the cause of my being led to provide for her myself. Whether or not she meant me to see that letter I shall never know. I shall not ask her. You will not. She owes no one her confidence."

Miss Gibbon did not give it.

"Father," said Constance, in sudden consternation, "have we repaid the money?"

"Of course we have. Or rather I have. What would you suppose?"

"I admit I had not thought of it."

"No, the power to think does not play much part in your relation with things."

"Father, you know you were not thinking of Miss Gibbon. What made you say that a woman sent the money?"

"Miss Gibbon sent it through me," said Miles, in an almost bewildered tone. "What am I to say to you? Who else was the instrument?"

"Father, I wish we could have the honest answer."

"Well, have it then," said Miles, in a sudden outburst. "I said it was a woman, to put you all off the scent. You would not expect me to help you on to it, would you? When I wanted to conceal something, and knew it was best concealed? Ellen, my dear one, you are troubled by this kind of talk. These are not questions that could be asked from your level. You had your own words to say, and it is to those we must give our ear. They were true words, my wife. You and I both failed to judge aright. We were without each other and the help we had come to depend on. We pursued a wrong course, each of us stumbling along alone. And I believed you were dead, when I made the effort to mend my life. I saw it as finally broken. No one seems to realise that, though we all believed it. And it is the answer to everything. The memory goes the deepest with me, as indeed how should it not? Now we shall go on together till death do us part. And we need not turn our eyes behind."

"As it is an unnatural direction," said Malcolm.

"We owe a great deal to Miss Gibbon and Malcolm," said Constance.

"We owe it to the Hand from which we take everything," said Miles, gravely. "Miss Gibbon and Malcolm were the instruments. And as such we salute them; they were chosen.

178

But we recognise the higher force. My wife, we will do so in our own way. We will go and be alone. We will even go from each other. We will meet when we have put the past behind, and can turn to the future and go forward."

"So Father is safe with himself," said Audrey, looking after them.

"And we are all safe with him," said Ursula. "He has given us what help he could. We looked to him for it."

"And he owed it to you," said Malcolm.

Verena suddenly broke into tears and ran out of the room, and Malcolm followed her.

"Well, what a story!" said Ursula. "And what characters it has in it! Or what a—hero!"

"Yes, we will not use another word," said Constance.

"Father was happy with Verena?" said Audrey, with a sound of question.

"We cannot say he was not," said Constance. "And we have to say that we wish he had not been."

"What had he in his mind, after he knew the truth?" said Ursula. "We can only ask the question, and not wait for an answer. I believe he thought he could continue in his course, or contrived to think so."

"Which did he love better, Mother or Verena?" said Audrey.

"Yes, we must say it once. Of course it was different. Of course we can see it was. I suppose he could have been happy with either, like the man in the song. But he thinks now that he is happier with Mother, or we will hope he does. Of course he cannot be at this moment, and knows it."

"And so is not having the moment," said Audrey. "Did Verena want to be revenged on him?"

"Yes, on him and on Mother. And she had her wish. But revenge, like other things, may be best in anticipation. Father tried to carry off the position, and that was so startling that he almost did so. It was an impossible effort, and made in an impossible way. And it showed that all things are possible."

"I am afraid we shall never feel the same to him again," said Constance.

"We shall feel we understand how we always felt to him. That will not be fair to him, but it is outside our power. Miss Gibbon, you often hear you are one of us. What do you think of the family to which you belong?"

"It is not for me to judge anyone. And I had a strange part to play myself."

"You had a noble part," said Audrey. "We are proud of the relationship, and wish you could be."

"Poor Father!" said Constance. "Do we begin to want to make excuses for him?"

"I hope so," said Ursula. "He needs them to be made."

"What does Mother feel about him?" said Audrey. "Will she ever say?"

"I suppose she will not. And it would tell us nothing. We can never know."

"We can hardly help feeling sorry for Verena," said Constance.

"I think I can," said Ursula. "She was jealous of Mother, and tried to spoil her life with Father, when Mother had suffered all she had, and done her no harm. And we cannot know how far she had succeeded. Such efforts do not completely fail. I think it would be wasting pity."

"Will people outside the family know about it?" said Audrey.

"Yes," said Malcolm, returning to the room. "And know more than there is to know. Though it seems that ought to be enough."

"I hope you do people injustice," said Constance.

"There is no ground for the hope."

"We should not want to exaggerate such things, if they concerned other people."

"Indeed we should. We are not without a tendency to do so, as they concern some of ourselves."

"Malcolm is joking," said Miss Gibbon.

"It is hardly the occasion," said Constance.

"I agree that it is not," said her cousin. "I should not joke."

"You all have to try to show courage," said Miss Gibbon.

"And I am managing too well?" said Malcolm. "Such effort can be too successful."

"Courage must surely be a good quality," said Constance.

"It can be taken to point to a lack of other qualities."

"It often is," said Ursula. "When people are brave in trouble, other people say how easily they have got over it."

"That is not saying anything against them," said Constance.

"Indeed it is. But they will not say we have got over this. They will assume that our heads are bowed for life."

"None of you has done anything to be ashamed of," said Miss Gibbon.

"It is a more humbling kind of shame, when you have had no choice in the matter."

"What does Father think about Verena?" said Audrey. "I mean about what she has just done?"

"He has not thought," said Malcolm. "He has had to think about himself. And he will not say in my hearing. And neither will any of you."

"We should not have dreamed of it, Malcolm," said Constance.

Malcolm turned to the window.

"My mother is here. The occasion runs its course. The power to keep away must have been left out of her."

"I suppose the boys are not with her?"

"Why do you suppose so? It is hard to break a habit. And they would not choose this juncture for doing so."

"They cannot know anything about this last—disclosure. There is no way in which they can have heard."

"There is always a way," said Malcolm.

Eliza's manner, when she entered, revealed that there had been a way.

"My dear ones, I felt I must come to you. Why do we give our reasons? It was just that my heart went out to you, and I followed where it led."

"As it was in the right direction," said Malcolm. "Perhaps you can receive news from a distance like a savage. It may be a power that education destroys. You did not have too much, and my brothers do not profit by it."

"What are you talking about?" said Eliza.

"About your unusual powers."

"Well, I do not think I am quite without them. My power of sympathy is great. And my awareness of troubles and pity for them as my own. You will all come to know it. You would know it already, if I were a person who had full justice. Why, Miles and Ellen, it is good to see you together, and to know there are bonds that nothing can break. I felt that there were. I told myself to be sure of it. But it is good to see the proof before my eyes, and before these others eyes that need it."

"Is Mother doing her best?" said Nigel. "Might not a direct attack bring more result?"

"Attack on what?" said Miles. "Oh, I heard you. I am prepared for you now. So you have heard something, have you, though you cannot know what it is? And I daresay you do know. I see you do. You need not try to hide it. I don't care what you know."

"That seems so aloof from us," said Rudolf to his brother, "when we care so much."

"Something else to amuse you! Something to put some interest into your lives! That is the purpose of everything."

"I feel it is one of the purposes. Anyhow it is a result."

"I suppose your lives are so drab, that you must clutch at the details of other people's."

"Is this a detail? Surely I were an ingrate to call it so."

Miles did not call attention to the debt to himself.

"I suppose your housemaid knows the postman, or perhaps you know him yourselves."

"I shall seek his acquaintance," said Nigel. "It is probably to be desired."

"What are you laughing at?" said Eliza. "It seems to be a grave occasion. I don't know how to explain it."

"Well, no one else knows," said Ursula.

"Oh, Eliza, if you do know, don't pretend you don't," said Miles. "We can see you know. We know you know. Of course you know everything. And we don't deny it. I don't deny it. I deny nothing. I have had some hard experience, of a kind quite beyond your grasp. And I have done my best with it. And my best was only what it was. I am only what I am. I don't pretend to be anything else. And you don't pretend to be either. Or, when you do, the pretence is poor enough. I often wish you would make a better one. That is all I have to say. It is all there is to be said."

"I think it is enough, Miles," said Eliza.

"How I hoped it was going to be some more!" said Rudolf. "I was holding my breath."

"Then hold it," said his uncle, casting him a glance. "Then you will be dumb."

"I had heard something, it is true, Miles," said Eliza, in a quiet tone. "But that is not knowing everything. If you want me to know, you must tell me."

"I do not want you to. I hoped you never would. Or I should have, if there had been any hope. But you have managed to somehow. I don't how. I don't want to know. I don't want to know anything. I refuse to know. And I refuse to say anything. And I will not, and there is an end of it."

"Where is Verena?" said Eliza, looking round.

"She is not down here, and will not be. Did you suppose she would? Would she choose to come and face you all, when you know what you do, and she knows it? Oh, you may be sure she knows. The hardness of you women to each other! Have you never made a stumble? I would rather be what I am, a weak, erring man, weaker than a woman I daresay, than a hard, hardly-judging person, who speaks with a second purpose all the time, and a malicious one at that. I bear no one ill-will, though something has been exposed, that I meant to be hidden, that had better have been hidden, as so many things in our lives had better be. Oh, I have not so much fault to find with myself."

"But we hardly expected so much praise," said Rudolf.

"Ellen, is there anything at all I can do for you?" said Eliza, turning from her brother-in-law. "If there is, you will tell me?"

"If there was, I should like it done. But I know of nothing."

"You have come through a strange passage in your life."

"Yes, it has made me see how seldom life is that. It is everything else, sad, hard, happy, anything it may be, seldom strange."

"It is a good thing you are equal to so much."

"I hardly feel I am equal to much more."

"And you will not have to be, my dear one," said Miles, in his louder tones. "You shall have nothing more on you at all. You shall face no one, say a word to no one, certainly answer no one. You will remember it, Eliza?"

"I have been feeling I must not remember what you say, Miles."

"Then act on it without remembering. You ought to be equal to it by yourself."

"My poor boy," said Eliza, turning to Malcolm, "you have had your share of it all."

"And you will see what it is," said Malcolm, looking at the door, as there was a hand upon it. "I have been waiting for the evidence. And it is here."

The door opened and Verena entered in outdoor clothes, and stood just within it.

"Why, is this a plan?" said Eliza.

"No, I hardly think so," said Constance.

"No, I was listening at the door," said Verena. "I have come to say good-bye, while you are all here. I did not want to feel I had not said it. I have not disliked all of you, and I shall not see any of you again. I am going to my mother's people, and I shall never come back. I cannot live the life I am expected to live in this house. I cannot see myself as I am seen here. I cannot suffer things that are not even seen as suffering. When Mrs. Mowbray came back, you all thought a part of my life did not exist. She thought of herself and her sacrifice, when she had decided not to make it. She saw her own trouble, and did not see that when hers was over, mine had begun. She never thought of what I felt for Miles, what I had come to feel when I was with him. I was to forget my very self, and live my life as a part of hers. Is it any wonder that I wanted to show her where she stood, to prove that Miles chose a life with me rather than with her? I saw his face when he hid that envelope, though he did not know I saw, and I did not guess at that moment what it was. No one thought he made any sacrifice, suffered any loss. I know he has seemed to recover, but it would have been the same, if he had not. Everything was to be as if it had not been. I have said it now, and I am glad it is said. If I had not cast off the burden, I should have carried it always. Now I am at peace, and I can put this life behind. Malcolm can divorce me when the cause is given. There is someone who will help me to give it, and will give me himself and what he has. Then Malcolm can marry Ursula, and she can bring up the child. A demand can be made on her as well as on me. And she will be equal to it. She is the best of you all. I know she dislikes me more than any of you do, but I see she is the best. And you will never see me again. You can forget you ever saw me. And you need not remember that there are things I shall never forget. You will not remember. I know you, though you have not known me. You will never know me now, and it is better that you should not. You are good enough for it to trouble you. And it would do nothing for me. I am good enough to be troubled too. Miss Gibbon will send my clothes after me; she has experience in sending clothes." Verena half-smiled as she broke off and shut the door.

Its sound came upon a silence. Miles stood uncertainly and then followed her, in the manner of a host attending a guest. Eliza made a movement to go after him, but was checked by Malcolm. In the hall Verena's voice continued, too low to be heard.

"Miles, you feel I have betrayed you. But how often have

you betrayed me? Your life since your wife returned has been a betrayal. I had to take something for myself, take something from her, before I left you. And I shall give you what is mine to give. You will have the child. Malcolm and Ursula will bring it up, but to you it will be yours and mine. There will be something of me in this house where I must leave a memory. There will be that between you and me. I can leave you more easily for knowing it, and for knowing how much more I have cared for you than you for me. I leave no broken heart behind. If there is one, I carry it with me. I shall keep the secret always. You will keep it as long as you feel the need. And while there is the thing that binds us, we do not utterly part."

Miles stooped and kissed her, and led her to the carriage, realising as he saw it, that she had laid her plans, remembering that she had always laid them. He hardly paused before returning to his family.

"Malcolm marry Ursula!" he said, as if he must voice the idea. "Well, I have never thought of it. And I don't mean it could ever happen. But I suppose I might have done so, and schemed and striven for it. Well, I am myself and cannot be anyone else. And I sometimes think I am different from other men."

"I sometimes do too," said Nigel.

"I thought of my own suffering," said Ellen, as if she had not heard. "It is true that I did. It was too much for me to forget. It is not true that I did not think of hers. I saw it and thought it best not to see it. I still think it was best. I shall always think of my trouble and hers, perhaps in that order, but never only of mine. As she has said, nothing ever dies."

"Ought we to go after her?" said Constance.

"It would be of no use," said Eliza. "She would not hear us. We should be doing it to do the right thing ourselves. And there is not any good in that."

"Neither is there, Eliza," said Miles, in a tone of approbation. "You put it well."

"It is the future we must think of," said Constance. "It is useless to pursue the past."

"It is needless," said Audrey. "It will pursue us."

"Oh, not for so long," said her father. "It will die away. We will not use words for their own sake."

"No threat is left behind," said Malcolm.

"None at all," said Ellen.

"Neither is there," said Miles. "It was open and clear when it ended. And how she looked, all alight, and flushed with fire and life! Yes, well, we will remember her at that moment."

"I would rather remember her at others," said Constance.

"We shall none of us forget her," said Audrey.

"No," said Miles, looking down, with a flush creeping over his face. "But remembrance will fade and grow dim. It will be overlaid. And we need not regret it. It is as it has to be. Much is already a memory."

"Very much," said Nigel. "And there has been some to add to it to-day. Suppose we had been there when the picture emerged complete! Uncle supporting one wife and arranging to marry another."

"I could not have borne it," said Rudolf, "either for myself or for him. And to think he endured it himself! He will always be a person who has suffered great things. If suffering is ennobling, he must be exalted by now. And I have found myself admiring him."

"What is that?" said Miles.

"We were wondering if suffering was ennobling, Uncle," said Nigel.

"Yes, well, I think it may be. I think it draws one upwards. I hope we may feel it does."

"I said it was ennobling," said Rudolf.

"But that was not all," said Miles, not yet raised above the level of mistrust. "What were you really saying?"

"Nothing, Uncle. We were just imagining a difficult moment."

"You will both go home," said Eliza. "I will have no

more of it. Malcolm and I will follow later. He is coming to stay with us for a time. You will go at this instant, and will not say good-bye. No one wants to hear another word from you."

"Well, here is a thing!" said Miles, leaning back and narrowing his eyes on his nephews. "Two great, grown young men sent home like a couple of schoolboys! And by a woman too! Well, this is an awkward moment, if you want one. I declare I am embarrassed myself."

"Uncle is having his revenge," said Rudolf.

"Revenge for what?" said Miles.

"For any awkward moments of your own."

"Ah, well, I have had my share of them. I remember my youthful agonies. And I don't think anything in later life quite comes up to them, or makes one squirm as they did. I daresay you are both squirming now. How one wished the floor would open and swallow one up! But if it did, there would be nobody left, I suppose. The moments come to all of us. Yes, go with your cousins, my dears. And you go too, Malcolm. They have done no worse than usual."

"I think Uncle would be left," said Rudolf, as they went. "He would be kept for greater things. Indeed he has been, though he does not seem to know it."

"Well, this is an idea about Malcolm and Ursula," said Miles. "And I have never thought of it. Believe it or not, it is the truth. But the thing has been set on foot, and the leaven may work. It would be a good end to everything. It all seems to want an end."

"It would be well for it to have one," said Ellen. "It might bring one in another sense. I have always had the idea, especially since Malcolm has lived with us. And I do not doubt that Eliza has."

"Well, I never have. I asked him to come quite without it. I had no thought of matchmaking or of hoping that a daughter might take your place one day. And I have always wished I could imagine my descendants here. Well, I am an innocent.

I doubt if there has been such another. Ah, Eliza, you think I am not innocent. I see the glint in your eyes. You are as bad as your sons. I don't know what there is to choose between you. If I were asked to pick the best or the worst of you, I should be hard put to it; and I tell you plainly."

"I did not wish you to tell me at all, Miles," said Eliza.

CHAPTER XIV

"Well, this is a new experience for me. I do not often create an occasion. I am used to being uncertain in my approach and of my welcome. But to-day I carry the news, and carry it so gladly. I am to make you the gift of a son, and take from you that of a daughter. It is good when people serve themselves without harming or grieving others. And this is news without hurt or grief."

"Yes, that is its pleasant feature," said Constance. "It is not only good for the pair concerned. We expected it, Aunt Eliza, but you have a right to be the herald. No one would dispute it."

"But someone has seen the need to say it," said Nigel.

"You have the right indeed, Eliza," said Miles. "And we rejoice to give and take as you say. Come, my wife, you are not to lose your girl. It is no day of veiled sorrow for you. We know how you would hide it, if it were."

"So Malcolm and Ursula did not tell us themselves," said Miss Gibbon.

"Oh, I think that was a natural shyness," said Constance.

"And here is something else that is natural," said Audrey.

"So Uncle has noticed Aunt Ellen veiling her feelings," said Nigel. "Are people more perceptive over what is supposed to escape them?"

"The precautions taken are a help to them," said Rudolf. "And of course they have to be taken."

"So nothing can be hidden from anyone."

"No, think of what has not been hidden."

"I am always doing so. I cannot get it out of my mind."

"I do not want to. I so enjoy having it there."

"It was Verena who had the idea of the marriage," said Constance to Audrey.

"Yes it was," said Miles, in full, steady tones. "And it did not prevent Ursula's accepting it. It puts my girl where she is. It shows her place."

"There might be a more comfortable one," said Nigel.

"So you are both here to make a mock of what is beyond you."

"They will not utter another word," said Eliza.

"Are Ursula and Malcolm in love?" said Nigel. "It seems to fit in too well. But it is wise not to start with what is known to be transitory."

"What is that?" said Miles.

"I said the feeling between Malcolm and Ursula was not transitory, Uncle."

"Ah, no, it is not. It is a vital thing, based on truth, strengthened by early stumbles, strong for the future. And Ursula will have her mother's place one day."

"I am glad that Malcolm does not offer only himself."

"No, he does not. And he is glad not to do so. But what are you doing, talking when you were to be dumb? Do not let your mother hear you."

"No, we will not," said Rudolf. "Is Malcolm looking uncertainly at Ursula? Perhaps he does not see admiration in her eyes."

"He may see other things," said Constance. "He is to give her the charge of his child. There could be no fuller trust."

"And you are to keep your daughter, Ellen," said Eliza. "I see your great content."

"And I feel it, which is better."

"Yes, your feelings are in your eyes. There is no need to suppress them."

"And there has been need, Eliza?" said Miles. "Ah, I know what you suggest. You cannot conquer your impulses even at this moment. Between what you do not say, and what your sons do, it is no wonder you are doubtful of a welcome. I wonder it surprises you."

"Father, surely this is a pity to-day," said Constance.

"Well, it may be, but it is not my fault. You should say the same thing to your aunt."

"I do not wish anything said to me by my niece," said Eliza. "It is not fitting, and I will not have it."

"Then may I say it to you myself, Eliza? Then the matter is ended."

"Malcolm and Ursula are not very loquacious," said Constance.

"And now will hardly be so," said Miss Gibbon, smiling. "That is not the way to loosen their tongues."

"They say what they have to say, to each other," said Miles. "We will not come between them."

"We certainly do not wish to do that, Father."

"Is this the happiest moment in their lives?" said Nigel.

"It is not supposed to be," said Constance. "It is a step to other moments."

"We are baffling them all," said Malcolm to Ursula. "They are expecting something of us, that is not forthcoming."

"We take what offers, and see it as it is. It is not their idea of romance. And they do not suspect it may not be ours either."

"We have been involved in enough, and seek it no further. Not that I could have lived apart from you or without our friendship. I did not think of it, even at the other time."

"Why is this not romance?" said Rudolf.

"It surely is," said his brother.

"Then we must fear it will not last. And it does seem much to expect."

"It will last," said Ursula. "So perhaps it is not romance. It is what we have in its stead, and it suits us both."

"Rudolf," said Nigel, in a low tone, "has Ursula always had a romantic feeling for Malcolm?"

"You should never suggest that the stronger feeling is on the woman's side. It is not the mark of a man. Of course I cannot suggest it."

"Mother says she thinks she has."

"That may be the mark of a woman. But I think it is that of an aunt."

"There is supposed to be full confidence between them. And there has had to be in their case."

"Oh, you know the world, do you?" said Miles. "Then you know that confidence may not involve so much."

"I have suspected it, Uncle. But then what is the good of knowing the world?"

"Have you ever met anyone who did not know it?" said Constance.

"You mean you know it yourself?"

"Well, I do not think there is much that would surprise me."

"I daresay not," said Miles. "Not after all you have seen. I mean that experience may go as deep in a quiet life as in any other."

"I suppose our life has been quiet," said Ursula to Malcolm, "but it hardly seems to be the word."

"It will be quiet now. We may have to remind ourselves that it moves at all. We can do nothing for it. There is no chance of a separate house."

"No chance of what?" said Miles.

"A separate house, Uncle."

"Oh, Ursula does not want one. She would not leave her parents. That is your old obsession. Cannot you put it behind you with the rest of the past? Or keep it in your mind without thrusting it into other people's?"

"We should miss you both, if you left us," said Constance. "Ursula has been my companion since before I remember."

"That should settle the matter," said Miles. "And I am sure it does for Ursula. As her father I can vouch for it."

"We should stay on the place," said Malcolm.

"No, you would not. There is no house for you on it. I do not know where you would be, if you cannot tell me."

"Well, we know where we shall be, Uncle. And you do not need telling."

"May I say how glad I am of the engagement, Malcolm?" said Constance. "I have always wanted a brother."

"Well, I hope Ursula has," said Miles. "Because she will have more than one. And I am not sure that I envy her."

"I wonder if Malcolm has wanted sisters," said Eliza.

"Oh, do not let us go on to dangerous ground," said Constance.

"Poor boy, he has wanted a wife," said Miles. "And he has found it hard to come by one. He has moved by steps to this happy stage. And it is the better to see him there."

"How seldom occasions turn out as we expect!" said Constance. "I can hardly think of one that has developed as I imagined it."

"And you can think of a good many," said Malcolm. "And some have certainly taken an unexpected turn."

"No one can speak in this house without meaning too much," said Nigel.

"Oh, nonsense," said Miles. "You are not used to meaning anything. And so you are struck by the difference."

"Well, it is time for us to go," said Eliza. "The occasion is soon at an end. It has not been what I expected either. But it is the forerunner of others, and some may fulfil our hopes. Ellen, it is the better to be with you, that we know the sadder thing. And you are the person I shall carry in my thoughts."

"I feel I shall sometimes have Verena in mine," said Constance to Audrey.

"And we shall be in hers. She said she did not dislike us. She seemed surprised by that. And I found myself feeling grateful for it. And she would hardly forget her time in this house. It was not an ordinary one."

"What was not ordinary?" said Miles.

"Oh, a time in someone's life, Father."

"Now listen to me," said Miles, lowering his voice and glancing in the direction of his wife. "Do not be always looking back. It is an unnatural and unlikeable habit, and it has an element of something worse. Look before you; welcome the future; lend your ears to the message that it brings. If I can do that at my age, you surely can at yours."

"We cannot always follow your example, Father," said Constance.

"Yes, you can, and you always could have, if you had been in my place. I am not different from other people. The theory has arisen from my strange life. And there you are again with your eyes on the past. It is impossible to break you of it. Yes, I am coming, Ellen. I will see Eliza out."

"There are things that we do tend to look back on," said Audrey.

"They hardly seem true any longer," said her sister.

"They never had truth. They depended on our not knowing it. And they had less, when they went on when someone did know."

"Mother," said Constance, when Miles had gone, "you will not mind a question? Would you have married Father, if you had known what was before you?"

"When people say someone will not mind a thing, they know he will," said Malcolm.

"Few of us would live at all, if we could foresee our whole future," said Ellen. "There are things beyond bearing in every life. We cannot escape them."

"You have not answered my question," said Constance.

"I think she has," said Ursula, "anyhow further than could be expected."

"It was surely a simple one."

"It was," said Malcolm.

"It is natural to feel a wish to know."

"And, as often in that case, hardly to express it."

"I think it is making too much of things to shrink away from them, as if they were humiliating."

"It may be the natural way to meet them," said Ellen, almost smiling. "That is why people appear to ignore them."

"It seems it would be healthier to speak easily of them to those near to us."

"You hint at the dangers of family life," said Audrey.

"I hint at nothing. It is not my way to hint. And I daresay we all feel the same at bottom."

"Why do you think that?" said Malcolm.

"Well, we will not become argumentative."

"People never say that until they have done so."

"A little healthy discussion need not be given that name."

"It tends to deserve it. And why should it be healthy?"

"Malcolm, glad though I am to welcome you as a brother, I do not regret that Ursula is to be your wife."

"I will try to do the part of a brother to you. I am sure I have been talking to you like one."

"I think there is a change in Malcolm," said Constance, smilingly resting her eyes on him. "There is something settled and satisfied about him at last."

"I am sure there is no change in Constance," said Audrey.

"Ursula," said Malcolm, moving away from the others, "I have had a secret from you."

"I thought you might have. I wondered if you knew it. Did Verena know you knew?"

"I think she did. We never spoke of it. She could not help it and could not alter it. Has anyone else guessed?"

"Only Mother. And she wants it to be kept from other people."

"So you and I are on equal terms. The child will not belong to either. That will help us to do our best for it. But we shall have to see your father doing his, and see Constance admiring him."

"I shall only be glad of that. She has not always done so. And I am half-glad he is to have something from the phantom life. He is accepting the old one well. We will not grudge him the one thing from the other."

"What does your mother feel about it?"

"It is no good to ask or guess. She may hardly know herself. She does not strive where she is helpless. And she must have known the risks of rising from the dead."

"Well, she knows them now," said Malcolm.

"Who knows what?" said Miles. "Oh, no one and nothing, I suppose."

CHAPTER XV

"Ah, this is a great day to me," said Miles. "The day when my daughter returns to the house where she will rule when I have left it. Pleasure is deepest when it depends on our dear ones rather than ourselves. I look to the end of my life with a settled mind. I shall live on in my grandchildren, here where I was born, bred, look to die——"

"You are quoting a poem, Father," said Constance.

"No, I am not. The words came into my head of their own accord. And I never quote other people. I use my own words or none. I should have thought you would know that."

"We believed we did," said Audrey. "And we were surprised to find our mistake. That does surprise people."

"Well, I suppose the poet and I said the same thing. We might easily do that. I mean we might by chance. I don't suppose there is so much difference between poets and ordinary—and other people. Well, we see there is not."

"It is a woman in this case," said Constance.

"A poetess?" said Miles, as though hardly accepting this as an authentic term. "Well, of course I was not quoting her. I am sure I was not."

"Have you any objection to quoting a woman?" said Miss Gibbon.

"I should not quote anyone. And naturally I should not quote a woman. What man would?"

"A man did," said Audrey.

"Would a woman quote a man, Mr. Mowbray?"

"Well, I suppose so, if she quoted anyone. She would not quote another woman. We can be sure of that."

"So women have not much success in the matter of quotation."

"Well, they have other kinds of success."

"And in this case this one, Mr. Mowbray."

"Yes, the poet was Christina Rossetti, Father," said Constance.

"Rossetti was a man," said Miles, in a manner of meeting success himself.

"Christina was his sister."

"Oh, he had a sister? Well, that was different. I suppose it ran in the family. That proves what I said."

"I do not know why, Father. But why not keep to your own interests? As Malcolm's child is a girl, you may have a grandson to succeed you. And I have an impression that you feel a bond between yourself and his daughter. She may need your protection the more, that she is not your grandchild. She will have no mother in the house."

"She will always be my charge," said Miles, in a grave tone. "She is in an uncertain place, though my Ursula will fulfil her trust. She is a reminder of something that passed through my life to pass from it, of a help that came to me when I had no help, a reminder of Malcolm's boyhood days. Her claim is the stronger that it is not a recognised one, that by some it would not be accepted. Ah, the little one is safe under my roof."

"The rooms must be ready for the travellers," said Miss Gibbon. "I have been clearing out the cupboards. There are some clothes of yours in one of them, Mrs. Mowbray. Shall I have them taken to your room?"

"Yes, I put them there when the rooms were not used, and I was short of space. But there are some drawers at the top of that chest, where I cannot reach, where they can go. They are not things I often use."

"None of us can reach those drawers," said Constance. "We shall have to enlist Everard's or Father's aid. That chest must have been designed for giants."

"For my grandfather, who was very tall," said Miles. "I can put your mother's things in it, and reach them when she wants them. Ask me at some other time. I cannot apply myself to these little tasks. They seem to baffle me somehow. I can't help putting them off."

"But Malcolm and Ursula will not put off their return, Father. You will have to bring yourself to this one."

"Oh, I will do it later in the day. It will only be a matter of a moment."

"Perhaps you can be spared the effort, Miles," said another voice. "You are not disposed to see virtue in your nephews, but to-day may be an exception. They can reach to any height for you. They have both grown up to you and beyond."

"Oh, I have begun to stoop. They are not really taller than I am. How are you, Eliza? Of course we expected you to come. There is no need to ask you. It is a settled thing."

"It is fortunate that it is. We should miss many family occasions, and be missed on them. It has become one of those things that seem to elude words."

"Then let it remain one of them," said Rudolf.

"I think Nigel is taller than you are, Father," said Constance. "Rudolf is about the same height."

"Oh, I can reach the chest as well as either. Come up, both of you, and see how your uncle compares with you. Miss Gibbon will give us the things to be put aloft. And I will wager I can reach beyond you both."

"Shall Audrey and I come to help fold the things?" said Constance.

"There should hardly be need," said Eliza, with a laugh. "Four people, three of them able-bodied men, will manage to carry some clothes across a passage."

"I said 'fold them', Aunt Eliza. That is hardly a man's province."

"Yes, I am as able-bodied as my nephews," said Miles. "Forty and more years older and equal to them! I question if they will be as strong at my age."

"There will be no demand on strength," said Eliza. "The heights are as Constance said."

"Well, we will let Father show his prowess," said the latter. "He has a right to prove himself in his own house."

"My dear, what an exaggerated way of putting it!"

"Well, put it in any other way. We do not want to disagree to-day."

"Or on any other day surely."

"It seems to be on most days," said Audrey.

"Miss Gibbon, provide us with our freight," called Miles. "And witness our power to hoist it aloft. Boys, come and carry the things for Miss Gibbon."

"This is a claim on my manhood," said Nigel, as he took the clothes to the room of his uncle and aunt.

"Well, manhood concerns itself with feminine needs," said Rudolf. "It is an accepted feature of it."

"I will get the drawers open," said Miles. "I can reach them as well as either of you. The empty ones are at the top. And they are not quite empty. There are some things already in them. I will take them out and make room for these. We can deal with the others later."

He did so, and his nephews and Miss Gibbon looked at the things revealed.

They were some night clothes of Verena's, thrown anyhow into the drawers, and unthought of since. They were of a kind to be chosen for an occasion, were marked with her name, and had been in use.

The silence was broken by Miss Gibbon.

"These are not Mrs. Mowbray's," she said, keeping her eyes on them. "I will have them put in order and sent to— where they belong."

"How did they get into the drawers?" said Nigel.

There was a pause.

"So you need to ask!" said Miles, in a charged tone. "Why do you not appear to know? What has come to your opinion of yourselves? How do you think they got into them? You of all people should be able to imagine it. You will not expect my help."

"We shall not say anything about it, Uncle," said Rudolf.

"Of course you will not. You have not sunk to that. Even in my moments of contempt for you I have not thought it. Such infamy would hardly be human. It would be unfit to think of it, to speak of it in Miss Gibbon's presence. And you will not say there is something else unfit for her, because I will not have it said. Do you hear me?"

"Other people will, if you are not careful," said Nigel. "And that would not serve you."

"Oh, you are wiser than I, and I am in need of your warning."

"You were at that moment, and I am glad you are paying heed to it."

There was another pause.

"Well, let us put the clothes into the chest," said Rudolf. "It is not a thing that would take us long."

"And we must not give ground for suspicion?" said Miles in a sardonic tone.

"Delay would give rise to question, and so to other things."

"Now will you listen to me?" said Miles. "I have one word to say to you. I have borne enough. I have borne what no other man has borne, what cannot be fathomed by you who have borne nothing. I have suffered long miseries of every kind. And I will suffer no further. Now that I am about to lead a just and loyal life in a respected place, I will be left unmolested to do so. Have you anything to say?"

"One thing," said Rudolf. "That we are relieved. You have reached the point of self-praise, and danger is past."

"Oh, have I?" said Miles, with a hint of a laugh. "Well I am sure I shall have no praise that I do not give to myself."

"Few of us have much from other sources."

"Ah, no, I daresay not. And I think I deserve a little, if no one else does."

"Yes, we know you do."

"I did what I could for myself, because I had to," said Miles, in a sharper tone. "And because no one else thought of doing anything. I thought of other people more than they thought of me. I look back and see that I did. And few of us can say as much."

"Everything is in order now," said Miss Gibbon, "if someone will shut the drawers."

"Yes, that is the sort of speech to make," said Miles, as he obeyed. "A kind-hearted, large-minded speech, meaning more than it sounds to mean. I hope you both hear it with understanding. It is a good word for the last one. And it can be the last."

"We should like to say one more, Uncle," said Rudolf. "You thought you were on the point of marrying Verena. We know that is the account of the whole matter."

"Oh, well, it goes without saying," said Miles, in an almost nonchalant tone, as he turned and went with a striding step from the room.

"I see how it was," said Rudolf. "Verena fled from the house on the day when Aunt Ellen returned. She threw the things out of sight and reach, meaning to fetch them later. And then it went out of her mind. And there was enough to distract it."

"Or it did not go out," said Nigel.

"Yes, we know it did," said Miss Gibbon. "We know just where she stands. There is no need to give her a wrong place."

"Uncle admires you, Miss Gibbon," said Rudolf. "But he does not admire you enough. He directs his appreciation towards himself."

"You must wish there was no such thing as clothes," said Nigel.

"Well, they have given me the chance to do something for other people."

"I am sure no one could admire you enough."

"Now must you lag behind?" said Miles's voice. "There will be comments and questions. One of you thought to say it. And there is no ground for gossip."

"What a strange statement!" said Rudolf. "It is wonderful how we are refraining from it. I wish someone could know about us. I wish everyone could."

"Well, have you decided who is the tallest?" said Constance, as they entered the drawing-room.

"Yes. Oh, I do not know," said Miles. "We could all reach the drawers. Everything is in order now."

"And we only have to await the travellers," said Eliza.

"Yes, you will stay with us, Eliza. But must your sons do so? We shall be having their talk, and we hardly feel inclined for it. This is a serious occasion to us, this day when our daughter returns with her husband to the home that will be theirs for life, that they will share with us for our lives. I should feel happier without them, if you will not misunderstand me."

"Happily she will," murmured Rudolf.

"What is that?" said Miles. "No, you need not tell me. I have no desire to know. But you see it is beginning. Your mother must see what I mean. I am uneasy with you, and I make no secret of it."

"I wonder he does not, considering everything."

"Well, they can go, Miles," said Eliza, "though I think you make too much of things. It is their own fault for being so loquacious. Talk is so natural to them, that they go too far for their company."

"Well, talk is no trouble to me either. That is not what I mean. It is the kind of talk and the attitude behind it."

"Well, it is rather independent and pointed for ordinary people."

"That would make it better. And it would not be my description of it."

"Well, it is as well that it escapes you. That is what they intend, to do them justice."

"It does not escape me," said Miles, also concerned to render this quality. "I wish it did. Then I should not mind it. But I catch the hints and innuendoes all the time."

"Our mother is being loyal to us," said Nigel.

"Well, you need some effort on your behalf. And you will have no one else's. You had better go home. Malcolm will visit you to-morrow. And I will give you messages to your new sister-in-law.

"My mind is still full of my old one," said Rudolf, as they left the house.

"Mine is full of so much, that I hardly know how to deal

203

with it. It is a terrible thing that we cannot tell the truth to Mandy."

"There is one more terrible. I find that I can tell her."

"And break your faith with Uncle?"

"I said it was terrible," said Rudolf. "But I cannot break a deeper faith with her. Our word to her is different from our word to him. One is as nothing beside the other."

"Well, I look forward to the moment. And she will keep her own counsel."

"It is odd that we believe that, being as we are. But I find I do believe it. I have to, or I could not tell her. And we always feel that no one can be as bad as we are. And I suppose no one could be."

"Well, have you any news?" said Miss Manders.

"No news, Mandy, nothing to call by that name. Nothing to call by any name at all, something never to be mentioned. We are on oath never to reveal it."

"But you can tell me," said Miss Manders, in a tone of easy expectance.

"Yes, we find we can. Of course we could not do otherwise. And we need not fear to destroy your faith in human nature. We know you have none, and could not bear to have any."

"Well, it is no good to expect things of people. You only meet different ones."

"We have met them, Mandy. And it is true that we did not expect them."

"It is only one thing. Do not raise her hopes," said Nigel.

"One thing is enough, when it is on this scale."

Miss Manders heard it and found it enough, indeed found something besides.

"So that is what happened to the clothes. Miss Gibbon said the sets were not complete."

"You must not talk about it to Miss Gibbon."

Miss Manders said nothing.

"There is something in your eyes, Mandy," said Rudolf. "That is, there is something behind them."

"Well, a thought did come into my mind."

"It has come into mine. And there is another to support it. It was suggested by Constance, and so can have no harm in it. And we will hope Nigel will not understand. Uncle is resolved to make Malcolm's daughter his especial charge."

"Ah, yes, so that is it," said Miss Manders.

"So Uncle will carry a secret to his grave. And it seems he has a right to, when he was prepared to carry so many. And we share it, we will help him to keep it from other people. It is between him and ourselves."

"He thought it would be," said Nigel. "It shows he is better than we are."

"Yes, he sent us home, as if there was nothing between us. When we knew the remaining secret of his life! And when he knows what it is to have secrets divulged. What trust he has in us! It shows how worthy he is of trust."

"So you are still gossiping," said Eliza's voice. "I felt so alone in that house, that I could not stay. I can see Malcolm to-morrow. I cannot imagine what you find to talk about."

"I daresay not," said Nigel, in an incidental tone.

"You will tell me, Rudolf. No doubt it is nothing. But you will not be dull with your mother. She has had an empty day."

"It is certainly not much, just something Uncle said to Constance. He is going to take an especial interest in Malcolm's daughter."

"Well, that is good of him. I suppose it is to help Ursula. He would hardly want to suggest any thoughts of the past. And he will be hoping for his own grandchildren. Perhaps he is afraid of treating this other child differently."

"Oh, I daresay he is!" said Miss Manders.

MORE TWENTIETH-CENTURY CLASSICS

Manservant and Maidservant

Ivy Compton-Burnett

Introduction by Penelope Lively

Ivy Compton-Burnett's novels are profound studies of family life; they are both immensely funny and completely original. *Manservant and Maidservant* describes the petty tyrannies to be found in an upper-middle-class Edwardian household, and shows Dame Ivy's wit at its sharpest and her characterization at its most memorable.

'there is no doubt about her originality and the uniqueness of her world, and her mastery of a sinister comic vein, of which *Manservant and Maidservant* (1947) is a characteristic product' *Scotsman*

'There is nobody in all this writing world even remotely like her.' *Guardian*

Ethan Frome and Summer

Edith Wharton

Introduction by Victoria Glendinning

Edith Wharton (1862–1937) is probably America's most original and important female novelist. This volume contains two short novels, *Ethan Frome* and *Summer*, both of which outstrip their predecessors in the genre of American realism.

Memoirs of a Midget

Walter de la Mare

Introduction by Angela Carter

'This book is an authentic masterpiece. Lucid, enigmatic, and violent with a terrible violence that leaves behind no physical trace ... It may be read with a good deal of simple enjoyment and then it sticks like a splinter in the mind.' So writes novelist Angela Carter in her new introduction to Walter de la Mare's elegiac study of the estrangement and isolation suffered by the diminutive Miss M.

The Slaves of Solitude

Patrick Hamilton

Introduction by Claud Cockburn

'Mr Hamilton has the habit, the art, or the genius of writing in his novels about the most familiar scenes, the most threadbare experiences, as if they were being observed for the first time.' Stephen Potter

A seedy boarding-house provides a wartime haven for Miss Roach, a lonely middle-aged spinster. Romance, glamour, and finally tragedy enter her life in the shape of a handsome American serviceman.

Riceyman Steps

Arnold Bennett

Introduction by Frank Kermode

Bennett's reputation as a novelist waned after the publication of his great pre-war novels, *Anna of the Five Towns*, *The Old Wives' Tale*, and *Clayhanger*, but it was emphatically restored by the appearance in 1923 of *Riceyman Steps*, the story of a miserly bookseller who not only starves himself to death, but infects his wife with a passion for economy that brings her also to an untimely end.

Seven Days in New Crete

Robert Graves

Introduction by Martin Seymour-Smith

A funny, disconcerting, and uncannily prophetic novel about Edward Venn-Thomas, a cynical poet, who finds himself transported to a civilization in the far future. He discovers that his own world ended long ago, and that the inhabitants of the new civilization have developed a neo-archaic social system. Magic rather than science forms the basis of their free and stable society; yet, despite its near perfection, Edward finds New Cretan life insipid. He realizes that what is missing is a necessary element of evil, which he feels it his duty to restore.

'Robert Graves' cynical stab at creating a Utopia is a poetic *Brave New World* filled with much more colour and dreaming than the original *Brave New World* of Aldous Huxley.' Maeve Binchy

His Monkey Wife

John Collier

Introduction by Paul Theroux

The work of this British poet and novelist who lived for many years in Hollywood has always attracted a devoted following. This, his first novel, concerns a chimpanzee called Emily who falls in love with her owner—an English schoolmaster—and embarks on a process of self-education which includes the reading of Darwin's *Origin of Species*.

'John Collier welds the strongest force with the strangest subtlety . . . It is a tremendous and terrifying satire, only made possible by the suavity of its wit.' Osbert Sitwell

'Read as either a parody of thirties' fiction or just crazy comedy, it deserves its place as a twentieth-century classic.' David Holloway, *Sunday Telegraph*

'an extraordinary 1930 novel about love between man and ape. A very funny minor masterpiece.' *Sunday Times*

In Youth is Pleasure

Denton Welch

Introduction by John Lehmann

Denton Welch's writing, so much admired by Cyril Connolly, Jocelyn Brooke, and Edith Sitwell, has a purity of style that is completely without affectation. In this, his best novel, he gives a profoundly disturbing vision of the world through the eyes of his adolescent hero.

The Aerodrome

Rex Warner

Introduction by Anthony Burgess

Published nearly a decade before Orwell's *1984* shocked post-war readers, *The Aerodrome* is a book whose disturbingly prophetic qualities give it equal claim to be regarded as a modern classic. At the centre of the book stand the opposing forces of fascism and democracy, represented on the one hand by the Aerodrome, a ruthlessly efficient totalitarian state, and on the other by the Village, with its sensual muddle and stupidity. A comedy on a serious theme, this novel conveys probably better than any other of its time the glamorous appeal of fascism.

'It is high time that this thrilling story should be widely enjoyed again.' Angus Wilson

'It is a remarkable book; prophetic and powerful. Many books entertain but very few manage to entertain and to challenge at such a deep level.' *Illustrated London News*

Dead Man Leading

V. S. Pritchett

Introduction by Paul Theroux

An expedition to rescue a man missing in the Brazilian jungle becomes a journey of self-discovery for his son. Conradian in conception, the treatment in the novel of obsession, verging on madness, is strikingly original.

'a rich, original and satisfying book' *Spectator*